SHADOW WEAVER

SHADOW WEAVER

MarcyKate Connolly

sourcebooks
jabberwocky

Published by Sourcebooks Jabberwocky, an imprint of Sourcebooks, Inc.
P.O. Box 4410, Naperville, Illinois 60567-4410
(630) 961-3900
Fax: (630) 961-2168
www.sourcebooks.com

Library of Congress Cataloging-in-Publication data is on file with the publisher.

Source of Production: Maple Press, York, Pennsylvania, United States
Date of Production: October 2017
Run Number: 5010731

Printed and bound in the United States of America.
MA 10 9 8 7 6 5 4 3 2 1

For my child.

I cannot wait to share words and worlds with you.

CHAPTER ONE

The first time my shadow spoke to me, I was a mere infant in the cradle. They say that on the night I was born, even the stars fled the sky and the moon hid under a dark cloak. That I was a quiet thing, with a shock of black hair and eyes like glittering onyx. I did not scream like other newborn children. And I did not reach for my mother like instinct should have instructed me.

Instead, I held out my tiny arms and smiled at the shadow in the corner of the room.

And it smiled back.

It's my favorite sort of day: stormy. Rain pelts the mansion in a wild rhythm, and the shadows shiver between the trees outside my windows. Everything is cast in lovely shades of darkness.

Dar—my shadow—is restless beside me, pacing from one corner of the room to the other. *Kendra is late*, she says. *We should play a game outside instead. Can't you hear the shadows calling to us?*

While the offer is tempting, I want to see Kendra today. At thirteen, she is a year older than me, and her mother is a maid. We play together sometimes, but I've barely seen her since she began working in our mansion a couple of months ago. Mother only allowed me to play with Kendra before she was a servant; now she says it isn't proper to socialize with the help.

Except for Dar, I've never had many friends, and I miss having Kendra around. The Cerelia Comet blessed me with magic, and I was born with the talent of shadow weaving. When I was little, I kept myself entertained by crafting toys from the shadows and playing with the one tethered to my feet. Dar is the only shadow that is my friend. To most people, shadows are things that remain stuck to walls and floors, but for me, they become whatever I wish—tacky, like clay, or as thin as smoke. I can mold them all to my will. Now that I'm older, my shadow-craft has improved. Before me on the low table in the sitting room is an array of shadows I've plucked from the corners of the mansion. A dark teapot steams next to three teacups and saucers. A smoky tray holds real biscuits—shadows don't taste very good—and three carved wooden chairs wait for Kendra to arrive so we can all take our seats.

Mother is not aware that I invited Kendra to tea today. I do have other games I'd rather play with Dar and the shadows, but Kendra doesn't seem to like them much. So tea it is.

Dar settles at my feet for a few moments before we hear a sound in the hallway. Hope warms me, but it is only one of the other servants walking by. I sink into a chair as disappointment swells inside my chest. Kendra is nearly half an hour late. I know she has duties, but she could have come by for a moment or at least sent a note explaining her absence.

Perhaps your mother kept her away, Dar suggests. *She doesn't like to have you playing with the help anymore.*

"You're probably right," I scowl. My mother has no trouble keeping her servants busy. And she does her best to keep every-one away from me.

I sit up straighter. "Let's bring Kendra a gift. It might be fun to sneak down to the servants' quarters after dinner."

Dar curves into a smile on the floor. *Does this mean we can go outside now?*

I laugh despite the strange heaviness weighing on me. The storm has nearly passed, and the sun is disappearing beyond the horizon. Even now, tiny specks of light flicker among the shadows on our lawn.

I pick up a jar from a nearby shelf, and Dar and I hurry outside before Mother can scold me for playing in the damp weather. The darkness deepens around us as we enter the woods by my home, the shadows cast by the trees reaching their limbs toward us in welcome. My feet begin to move, and I weave between the moss-covered trunks while Dar hums a tune. Together we dance in the gloaming, coaxing shadows and fireflies into the jar. By the time the jar is full, I am breathless from laughter, but not enough to forget the hollowness that blossomed when Kendra didn't appear this afternoon.

"Emmeline!" My mother's voice stops my feet in their tracks.

"We better hurry or we'll be late for dinner." I secure the

4

lid on my jar. Dar sighs but follows, her shape angling toward the trees like she'd rather remain outdoors. When I close the door behind me, she is at my side again. Even if Mother does keep me from Kendra, I am never alone. I always have Dar to keep me company.

In the jar, the shadows swirl around tiny flitting dots of light. Kendra always liked pretty things, and these shadows are so lovely, I'm sure she'll like them too. I hope Mother hasn't been working her too hard. I slip the jar into a hidden pocket in my skirts.

"Emmeline!" Mother calls again.

"Coming," I call back, and hasten toward the dining room.

⟵ • ⟶

After dinner, Dar and I pretend to head for my rooms; then, when Mother and Father aren't looking, I cloak myself in shadows and we sneak down to the servants' quarters. Kendra and her parents share a room, and I've visited her there once or twice before. She is probably tired from a hard day and forgot all about our tea.

But when Dar and I hover outside her door, ready to

knock, I hear voices. My hand pauses inches away from the wooden slats. It is one of the older serving girls, and she and Kendra are laughing. A pang of jealousy shoots through me. Kendra has never laughed with me like that.

"Emmeline invited you to play tea? Even though she's twelve years old?"

I flinch. It isn't my fault we only play tea. Kendra refuses to play any other shadow games.

Kendra groans through the door, and I can picture her tossing her pale hair over her shoulders. "She's crazy. Shadow weavers may be able to make things from shadows—which is bizarre enough—but they're not supposed to be able to hear and talk to them too. None of the comet-blessed have more than one talent—everyone knows that. But she honestly believes her shadow is a living thing. She even talks to it and pretends it talks back. She's insane!"

Heat flashes over my entire body. I brace myself with one hand against the door frame. Their tinkling laughter feels like glass striking my eardrums. Dar growls.

I may be the only one who can hear Dar, but that doesn't mean I'm mad.

She isn't worth our time, Emmeline. She has a cruel heart. All those times she played and made nice when she really thinks you're crazy! Dar huffs. To them she is only a shadow stuck to the floors and walls, but to me she is so much more. *We're better off without her.*

The other serving girl finds her voice again. "Well, it's a good thing you didn't go. You know what they say about what happened to that neighbor girl, Rose."

Kendra's laughter tapers off. "Emmeline is just crazy enough to be dangerous."

My heart sinks all the way into the ground. I shift the jar of shadows in my hands, my palms suddenly slick, and the fireflies wink. The way the dark and light play off each other is beautiful, but I realize now that Kendra never would have appreciated this gift.

She didn't say a word hinting at her true feelings when the three of us played with my shadow dolls and drank tea from teapots made of smoke. It was a game she only pretended to enjoy.

She was never my friend at all.

"You're right, Dar." I climb back up the stairs to my rooms, and the heat begins to vanish, until all I can feel is cold.

Later that night, while Dar comforts me in my quarters, running her cool fingers through my hair and brushing the tears from my cheeks, the fireflies' lights go out. I curl into a ball on my bed and send the swirling shadows back to the woods, with a promise that from now on, I'll only share them with those who will truly appreciate them.

CHAPTER TWO

Dar buzzes with excitement as we wait around the corner of the back stairwell the servants always use. It is darker and dustier than the stairs in the main part of the mansion, which is why my shadow suggested it. We are always on the hunt for new games to amuse us. Today is no exception.

Kendra should be coming by any minute now. I've refused to acknowledge her existence ever since I discovered her true feelings. But today we will show her. Dar is real.

Sometimes I hear the other servants whispering about me when they don't realize I hide nearby, concealed in a web of shadows—the only way I can get close enough to get to know them. Dar assures me they're jealous. Most people don't have magic like I do. Once every twenty-five years, a handful are blessed with gifts when the Cerelia Comet passes over our lands. In the past, people like me were celebrated for their gifts, but over the years, those without magic have grown more resentful of my kind. Especially those of us with talents that aren't as inherently useful as growing plants quickly or controlling water.

I thought Kendra was different. She was one of the few people I could talk to in this house, one of the few who I thought had gotten to know me. But I was wrong. She is just like the others.

It is midday, but there is only one small window in this stairwell, and I've made sure to blow out all the candles. The darkness makes me bold, and Dar swells next to me as the minutes tick by on the old grandfather clock down the hall. My shadow is connected to me, but she can move and stretch better than any human.

Soon we hear it, the clip-clop of Kendra's too-big hand-me-down shoes carrying the weight of the laundry basket. Dar expands, waiting to be released. I hide in my corner and hold my breath.

Kendra passes us by without a glance in our direction. She

can barely see around the overflowing laundry basket as it is. Dar springs forth, shifting into a giant monster at the last minute, all dark teeth and gaping mouth. Kendra screams and leaps back, and the basket sails away and bounces, breaking in half. She lands awkwardly on one foot and stumbles to her knees, cursing under her breath.

Dar snickers, snapping back to my side, but my own laugh dies in my throat as I watch Kendra's face twist in anger. It isn't quite as funny as I'd hoped it would be after all.

"Did you have to change to your monster form?" I whisper, pouting. We'd planned for her to mimic my mother's shadow. Appearing when my mother wasn't nearby should have been startling enough.

But that's my favorite shape, Dar says.

"Next time, no monster. Stick to the plan," I whisper.

Dar sighs. *All right, I promise.*

With shaking hands, Kendra begins to put the scattered clothes into a pile. I step out from the shadows where I've been hiding.

"Can I help?" I ask, my hands fidgeting with the edges of my sleeves.

Kendra skitters back when she sees me, but one foot isn't working as well as the other now. She leans against the wall and whimpers. "Your tricks are awful, Emmeline," she says. "And so are you."

My face blanches and I turn away from her resentful gaze.

"Let's go," I whisper to Dar. She has swelled up to twice her normal size now. She loves to play games.

But we will miss the best part, she objects. Dar likes to relish her handiwork and watch the aftereffects of our games, but I have no taste for it today.

Heaviness fills my chest. I shake my head and scurry down our side of the hallway. Dar has no choice but to follow me. No servants stop me in my hurry; they keep their eyes down and move aside to let me pass.

I vaguely recall a time when the household staff would look me in the eyes. Back then, Mother and Father were not quite so distant as they are now. But that was before the incident. I've barely thought of it in years, but the conversation I overheard between Kendra and the other servant has brought it back to mind recently.

I was only six years old, playing hide-and-seek in the

forest on our estate with a neighbor's daughter, Rose, who was the same age as me. All I remember is dozing off in my hiding spot after Dar assured me she would keep an eye on the girl and make sure she'd never find me, leading her away from me and deeper into the forest. When I woke up, night had fallen, and the woods were crawling with a search party looking for us both. I returned safely home; Rose did not.

I cried for days, swearing to my parents that Dar had only intended to lead Rose away from where I hid. But she must have wandered too far.

Later, I overheard Mother and Father discussing it: as dusk fell, Rose had roamed deeper and deeper into the woods and somehow fell into a pond miles from where I had last seen her. Her family was devastated and moved away. My parents never looked at me the same way again. That was also around the time they began to suggest that I stop telling people that Dar is real.

I've been cloistered ever since.

Moments after I close the door to my room, there's a sharp knock.

"Who is it?" I call.

"Open the door, Emmeline," Mother says. My heart sinks. Did she figure out we played a trick on Kendra already?

I open the door, and Mother steps inside, skirts swaying and catching on the pile of shadow animals I shoved onto the bottom shelf of a bookcase by the door. One shaped like a puppy clings to the edge of her dress and trails after her as she takes a seat. She doesn't even notice. I pick it up from the floor and let it dance and wag in my palm.

"What are we going to do with you?" she says, eyeing the tiny shadow creature in my hand with distaste.

I frown and sit on the edge of my four-poster bed, which is decked in white lace just as Mother prefers, while Dar pools at my feet. She's sulking. We're going to get into trouble.

"What do you mean?" If Mother doesn't know about our game yet, I'm certainly not going to enlighten her.

But she gives me that look—the one that says she knows what I've done and why don't I just come out with it. I shrug.

"You cannot treat the servants like that, Emmeline. They are not your playthings."

My stomach twists. Drat. She does know.

Kendra must have told her, Dar murmurs. I'm sure she is right.

"I don't know what Kendra told you, but she doesn't like me. It was just a little fun."

Mother crosses her arms over her chest. "Your fun twisted Kendra's ankle. Your shadow tricks are not at all amusing."

My shoulders droop. We hadn't meant to hurt her.

"That leaves us with one less servant this week," Mother continues. "And we are expecting guests."

"We are? Who?" My ears perk up. Guests are rare. Mother and Father don't like to let anyone know about my shadowcraft if they can help it. Guests mean I might have someone new to talk to even just for a little while.

"An entourage from Zinnia is coming to discuss a possible treaty with our neighboring land Abbacho. They are trying to drum up support among the nobles for uniting us all under one rule and law." She narrows her eyes. "This is important. There must not be any incidents while they are here. Please do not embarrass us. No tricks, and no mention of your shadow."

Her words smart, turning my cheeks pink as though I've been struck. I stare at my hands twisting in my skirts. Embarrass them? With so few people around with magic talents, you'd think they'd want to show me off. But they don't see how wonderful the shadows are, the beauty in the darkness, not like I do.

Only Dar understands me.

She squeezes my ankle like she knows my thoughts. *You're not crazy, and you're not an embarrassment; you're a gift. Someday we'll prove it to them.*

I take a deep breath. "I will do my best, Mother. I promise."

CHAPTER THREE

The shadows seem thinner than usual today. Perhaps they've grown shy and shrink from the company slated to arrive this afternoon. Our last visitors came a couple years ago when we thought it would be fun to checkerboard the floor in the guest wing with shadows.

Their unpleasant daughter, however, had not agreed.

She hadn't wanted to play any games with me and turned up her nose at my shadow animals. When I tried to tell her about Dar, she laughed and told me I was too old for imaginary friends. Later that night she tripped down a flight of stairs that was obscured by the checkerboard shadows and broke her arm. The next morning, her family packed their things and left. I had only intended to make the guest wing fancier, not hurt her, but Mother and Father were furious.

Hopefully these new visitors will be nicer. I must do my best to obey Mother and not mention shadows at all. And if the guests *are* unpleasant, then I will spend as much time in my rooms as possible. Who needs them when I have Dar and the lovely darkness at my fingertips?

It's been ages since we've had anyone new to eavesdrop on, Dar purrs in my ear as we head down the hall toward the kitchens. *I've grown bored of listening to your parents and the servants. When these newcomers arrive, we should listen in on them to get a sense for what they're like.*

I smile. "I like the sound of that." Dar knows eavesdropping has long been my favorite game. When I listen to others talking, I can pretend I'm there in the open laughing with them—not hidden nearby in the shadows.

When we turn the corner to the main hallway, I pause in my tracks. Before me stands a strange little girl with ghostly hair floating around her face like a living thing. She tilts her head and furrows her brow at me. The fading yellow dress she wears is dirty around the edges of the hem and sleeves. Her eyes are something else—wide and staring, like she is taking everything in but not always registering what she sees.

Dar curls over my shoulder. *She's an odd thing.*

"Do you think she's lost?" I whisper back. "Have the guests arrived already?"

The girl breaks into a grin and claps her hands. "I know you," she says in a singsong voice. "You shimmer and shine no more." Then she stops and stares again. It feels like a cold hand grazes over my mind. Like the girl sees right through me. I shiver and call my shadows closer. Soon the safety of darkness surrounds me, and I can no longer feel the little girl's eyes. She doesn't react to my disappearing act at all. But as Dar and I slide down the hallway out of sight, the little girl still sings behind us: "I know you, I know you."

I can't get away from her fast enough.

←—•—→

When we reach the kitchens, we discover that I was right: the guests have arrived early, which means no time for us to have a little fun in the mansion first. Dar is disappointed, but I am not.

It is a cloudy day, perfect for wayward shadows in the woods on the grounds of our home. I sneak an apple tart from the cook, who only gives me a passing glance, and then leave the house behind. Once, after the incident, Mama and Papa forbade me from wandering alone in the woods, but they gave up on that long ago. The shadows call to me; I can't help myself.

I break into a run, Dar whipping behind me like a dark cloak, and head into the forest, leaving all thought of my parents' disapproving glares behind. The trees never judge me. I only stop when I'm far enough away that no one can see me anymore if they glance out the windows. I laugh, and throw my hands toward the sky. The air tastes like rain, and the wind slips through the branches, making the trees dance. It's the perfect day.

The shadows shimmy out from their places between the trees at my call, and I begin to shape them with my magic. They form a square that slowly distorts into an elongated diamond. Then I fashion a tail to the end of it. I craft the shadow string, holding it down as we head for the field at the edges of my parents' lands. The wind tosses my shadow kite into the air, and Dar and I take turns chasing each other up and down the hill.

We settle into our favorite spot at the top of a hill, the dark forest at our backs and the field stretching out for miles in front of us, and lie down to watch the storm clouds darken over our heads. At my command, the shadows at the bottom of the clouds make funny faces and form odd shapes. But I don't laugh as I usually do on days like this. One of the clouds curls into wisps, reminding me of the little ghostly girl's hair. She haunts my thoughts.

Don't worry, Dar says. *She is nothing.*

"That's what bothers me," I say. "She seemed so…empty. So…off." It unsettled me more than I want to admit. But I trust Dar. She can read people in ways I've never been able to. She's my best friend.

The clouds churn over our heads, and drops of water begin to pelt my face. I groan. "I suppose we must go. Mother and Father will be furious if they find me sneaking into the house soaked when we have guests. Especially ones as important as these."

They don't know what they're missing, Dar says as she shimmies between the raindrops.

I smile and release the shadows that formed my kite back

into the woods. They whisper around me for a moment, like friends only parting for a brief while, and then they're gone. Dar and I return to the house, the rain clouds chasing after us. But when we near the house, a flash of white catches my eye, and I pause. That strange little girl is just standing there, in the middle of the back garden, with the rain pelting down on her. She doesn't move, but she stares straight at me. From where she stands, she has a full view of the woods.

Was she…was she watching us? Did she see us go into the woods and just waited for us? But why?

I shiver when I realize her mouth is moving, forming the same words over and over. I don't have to hear her to know she is still repeating the same refrain: *I know you, I know you.*

I turn away and hasten past the garden, hoping she doesn't follow us. As soon as we reach the inside, we race up to my rooms.

←——•——→

I had every intention of heeding my mother's warning, but there is still another hour until dinner, and I can't help wondering about these strange visitors. Are they all like that girl? Odd and unsettling? All I know is that they are people my parents want to impress.

Cloaked in darkness so no one can see us, we leave my chambers and head for the guest wing.

Maybe they did something to make her that way, Dar suggests, and a chill runs through me. I hope that isn't the case.

Of course, now I must know. We haven't encountered her again since we came inside. The rain still pelts the exterior of the mansion, filling the house with echoes. It makes excellent cover for sneaking where I'm not supposed to be.

Playing tricks may be Dar's favorite game, but mine is eavesdropping. I've become very good at it over the years.

The door to the guest quarters is ajar. Dar and I and all the shadows I can muster wedge ourselves into a corner across the way so we have a good vantage point but can remain hidden. I'm certain my parents have not told them what I can do, not after Mother warned me to behave. No, they are hoping they don't find out.

Dar whispers in my ear. *Your parents would want to know if their guests had done something to hurt that girl. We'll find out what kind of people they are.*

With renewed determination, I settle into the corner and wait. Mother's finest paintings deck the halls of the guest wing. I prefer the old tapestries near my rooms. They have more story, less show. They also provide better places for playing hide-and-seek. But here, we have a direct line of sight into the living area where a few brocade-upholstered chairs surround a low table with clawed wooden feet. It isn't long before two strangers come out from a back room. The older man is tall with yellow hair and a close-cropped beard. Both men have a deeply tanned complexion, and the younger one has eyes so blue I can see them from here. But they sit with their backs to us, making it hard to hear what they say. All that reach us are low murmurs and occasional laughter.

We should get closer, Dar says.

"It's risky…" I murmur.

It's worth it.

It's cloudy enough outside that the meager light slipping in from the windows leaves room for deep shadows in every corner. Just the right size for me to squeeze into and mold the shadows around me. Mother and Father will never know. We tiptoe through the partially open door, only a moment before one of the men comments on how drafty it is in the house and gets up to close it. In my corner, I hold my breath, my heart pounding against my ribs. I can't get locked in here. I'll have to wait until they leave for dinner before I can make my escape.

"That's better," the younger man says as he returns to his chair. He appears to treat the other man with deference. The latter must be the lord my parents wish to please. His face is stuck in a permanent sneer, which makes it seem like he is not at all impressed with his accommodations. Poor Mother. She prides herself on the lush sitting rooms in our house, but it seems all the silk and brocade in the world would not satisfy this man.

"What do you think, Uncle Tate? Are Lady Aisling's instincts correct?" the younger man asks.

Tate sighs and swirls a dark liquid in the glass in front of him, but he does not drink from it. "That remains to be seen. If Simone is doing her part, we should know by morning."

"Is that where she's wandered off to?"

"She is well-trained." He sniffs the liquid in his glass, then wrinkles his nose.

"I don't know how you and Lady Aisling do it, but your little collection has the most well-behaved servants I've ever seen. Also the strangest."

Tate barks a laugh and sets the glass down on the table. "Well, Alden, that is a price we are willing to pay. And really, the credit is due to Lady Aisling's fine work. I am only her servant and messenger."

Their conversation troubles me, but I can't put my finger on why. The odd girl I ran into is a servant; so what?

"Not to mention her second in command and her best hunter. She gives you the leads, and you follow them. If Lady Aisling is right, Simone will sniff out another specimen here."

The hair on the back of my neck stands on end. Dar begins to balloon with agitation, but calms at my touch. I don't quite understand the meaning of the conversation, but I don't like it one bit.

A search of their quarters is definitely in order once they leave, Dar says.

The idea is very tempting. Father will be angry if I'm late for dinner, but I must get to the bottom of this. The more I hear, the more I am convinced that Dar is right and that they did something to that girl. She is nothing like them. Something is wrong here.

Before I can wonder where the little girl is, the door

opens, and she wanders in, her hair and dress still wet. I stiffen, hoping the shadows and Dar combined will be enough to keep me concealed. It almost seemed like she could see through them earlier, but no one ever has before. She meanders aimlessly around the room, even after the younger man—Alden—tries to greet her.

"Simone," Tate says sharply. Her head snaps up, and her blank stare rests on him. "What did you find out?"

A slow grin creeps over her face.

"They're here," she says.

My body freezes. She can't mean me. She hasn't even looked in my direction since she entered the room.

Don't worry; she's crazy, Dar says. I relax slightly, but my stomach is still a mess of knots.

The man frowns. "Where?"

Simone sticks out her hand and points directly at me. Tate and his friend follow with their eyes.

I can't move. I can't even blink. My insides clench.

The little girl fixes her unsettling gaze on my corner, looking me straight in the eye like my shadows make no difference.

"I know you," she says.

Before any of them can reach me, I muster up all the strength I have and throw every shadow in the room at the two men and the girl all at once. They fly toward them, some in ferocious forms, others like giant shards of shattering glass, all meant to distract.

Run, Dar says. I do.

CHAPTER FOUR

I only make it ten feet out the door before I run right into Father and Mother.

"Emmeline!" Mother says. "What on earth are you doing?"

I glance behind to see the two men and the little girl in the doorway, mouths agape. Though the older man now wears a wolfish expression that I don't like at all.

My stomach turns. I've been caught.

"This is your daughter?" Tate asks.

Father glares at me. "What did she do?"

"Nothing, I—"

"I wasn't talking to you, Emmeline," Father says.

My chin trembles, but I snap my mouth shut and huddle against the wall. I've disappointed them again. Dar creeps up behind me and encircles me in her arms. *Don't worry*, she whispers. *They'll forgive you.*

Will they? Mother and Father have gradually grown less and less tolerant of my magic. Somewhere along the line, I became an embarrassment and, I suspect, in their eyes, dangerous.

Tate steps forward. "Your daughter has quite the unusual talent." His eyes sparkle. "Though I'm sure it could be put to better use than eavesdropping on guests."

I stare at my feet. My entire body feels like it has been set on fire by the five pairs of eyes gazing at me.

"Emmeline," Mother says, her tone telling me exactly how she feels about my behavior.

I scuff my slippers on the cold stone floor. "Sorry," I mumble.

Father won't even look at me. "Go to your room. You will not be joining us for dinner after all."

I can't leave fast enough. But as I do, Tate's words echo after me: "My dear Curt and Melina, I have a proposition for you..."

←——•——→

We wait until dinner is long over and the newcomers have retreated to their quarters. Then Dar and I sneak out of my room. Mother and Father are already angry with me, but I must know what Tate meant about a proposition.

It sounded like he was referring to me. After what he said about hunting earlier, that makes me particularly nervous.

I will be in terrible trouble if they catch me eavesdropping again so soon after last time, but with that little girl nowhere in sight, I should be safe. It only takes a few minutes, and a duck or two into a corner to hide from a servant to reach their wing.

I hover outside my parents' bedroom. Soon the sound of their hushed voices warms my ears, the air crackling with their nerves.

Let's see what they're about, Dar suggests in her soft, lilting voice. Her dark form stretches and winds around me. Now I can get close to Mother and Father and they'll be none the wiser.

The shadows deepen by their door, and I flatten myself against the wall to hear better. Dar puffs out. She always gets curious when she suspects they're talking about her. Or rather, about me talking *to* her.

"We can't just do nothing, Melina. She's growing stronger. We won't be able to control her soon," Father says.

My mother sighs. "We could keep trying. If we can convince her to let go of the idea she can talk to the dark—"

"You know we can't. We've tried for years. And what worries me, and our gossiping servants more, is that she may be telling the truth. Who knows what kind of creatures might flock to someone with power like hers? We're not equipped to manage that."

The edges of Dar's form bristle. I reach out a comforting hand to smooth them over.

"But must we send her away? What if they're not equipped to handle her either?" Mother's voice cracks on the word *away*, and with it my heart.

Send me away? She must mean with Lord Tate. I shudder, remembering the expression on his face after he discovered my talent.

Dar fumes, and her form takes on a red tinge.

I hear my father pacing for a few more moments, each

step matching the hammering in my chest. "What else can we do? The servants are terrified of her. Tate is the first person to see what she can do and not fear her. Instead, he is offering us a solution."

The more I hear, the more my stomach roils with revulsion. I peek around the doorway to see my mother sitting on the edge of their bed and my father kneeling in front of her. His hands grip hers so tightly that his knuckles are bone white. Dar tightens around me, her version of a hug. It's the only comfort I can find.

"Melina, we must do this. Tate will cure her. He swears it. He presented the child he has with him as proof. Didn't you see how well-behaved she was over dinner? She followed every order without hesitation and remained quiet as a mouse. Not a hint of a talent in her anymore. Lady Aisling has truly devised a means of stamping the magic out. Lord Tate has found several children for the lady to help on his tour of Parilla. What kind of life are we condemning Emmeline to if we don't give her every chance to be normal? This is a chance for all of us to be free of this curse."

Tate's employer Lady Aisling cured that girl of magic? I

shudder. That must be what's wrong with her, why she acts so strangely. I can't imagine being stripped of what makes me, me.

I can bear no more. Not bothering to cloak myself with shadows, I run down the hall, Dar clinging as close as she can.

I close my bedroom door behind me and sink onto the window seat. When I pull the gauzy curtains aside, the stars wink hello. The night is a comfort. All the darkness and shadows crawling over our yard and woods belong to me. They're mine to bend and play with. My parents would take all that away.

Dar settles on the floor next to me. *They're fools*, she says. *They don't see how perfect you are, just as you are.*

I sniffle and wrap my arms around my knees. "I don't want to be cured. I don't want to lose my shadows. And I don't want to lose you."

Dar slithers up onto the window seat. *You'll never lose me.*

Tears sting my eyes, and the scene outside my window blurs. "Do you think it's true? Do you think this Lady Aisling can actually cure someone of magic?"

No. My shadow turns so dark I can no longer see through her. *Tate is nothing but a liar. There was still something very not normal about Simone.*

"What do you think they did to her?" I shiver at the memory of Simone's strange gaze.

Nothing good. There's a difference between breaking and curing.

Before I can respond, someone knocks on my door, startling me to my feet. "Emmeline? Are you in there?"

"Yes, Father," I say, quickly grabbing a book and curling up in the nearest chair. He opens the door and regards me steadily. No trace of regret in his eyes. Just finality. My heart sinks into my toes.

He pulls up a chair and sits across from me. "Emmeline, you have been offered a wonderful opportunity, and your mother and I have decided you will take it."

Opportunity? Is that what he calls it? Dar huffs.

"What kind of opportunity?" I ask warily, already knowing the answer all too well.

"Our guest, Lord Tate, feels for your...predicament, and he wants to help. He and his patroness Lady Aisling have taken many children just like you under their wings in Zinnia, and they've given them a chance for a wonderful life. All the advantages and education you could want."

35

Because that is just what every child wants, Dar says. I try to stifle my smile, but my father sees it and misunderstands.

"Good, I'm glad to see you smile. You will be leaving with him tomorrow. We will miss you, but you may come home on holidays. I know it will be the best thing for you." He stands, looking more relieved than he has a right to be.

"Wait." I grab his hand as panic boils over inside my chest. "What if I don't want to go? I want to stay here. I love it here. This is my home, my woods, my family. I don't need to go anywhere else."

His face settles into a stern expression. "Don't you want to learn how to be a proper young lady?"

My face blanches. "Well, of course, but—"

"Someday, you will inherit this estate. You cannot run it with your magic, and the servants will not continue to work here if they fear you. You have to learn some self-control. It is for the best."

"Please, don't make me go. I'll—" I swallow the lump in my throat. "I'll never use my shadows anywhere but in my own room or the woods again. I won't talk to Dar when anyone else is around. I'll—"

"Stop, Emmeline." Father pulls his hand out of my grasp. "This is not up for debate. Too much damage has already been done. Someday you will thank us." With that, he leaves and doesn't look back to see how his words affect his only child. When the door closes, it is like a death knell on the life I've loved.

"I don't want to go." My tears begin in earnest now. All the things I love would be left behind. The bottom shelf of the bookcase stuffed full of shadow toys inspired by the characters from my storybooks. The woods where I can run free and play with the shadows that live between the trees. My family, my home—everything I know is *here*. "What will I do?"

My shadow flares red for a brief moment, then curls around me. *I can help you, Emmeline. I can ensure you will never have to go anywhere with that man. But you must agree to help me in return.*

Hope kindles in my heart. I can always count on Dar. "Yes! Please! I'll do anything."

A darker patch of shadow curves into a smile. *You are too good for them. They don't deserve you. I will take care of it tonight. You needn't worry about a thing.*

My hope tempers. "Will I have to sneak out to the guest quarters?"

You won't have to do anything. I can stretch myself thin as a string while you sleep.

"I could hug you, Dar. Thank you," I say. "But what do you need my help with?"

Dar hesitates. *There is something I have never told you, Emmeline.*

"What do you mean?" A warm, prickly feeling crawls over my back.

I was not always a shadow.

My jaw drops. I have often wondered where Dar came from, but she has always sidestepped my curious hints. Is she a creature born from my magic or did she exist before I came along?

"How is that possible?" I ask.

I was once human, but now I am only a lost soul. I want to become flesh again. I want to live. Only a person like you, a shadow weaver, can help me. Then we'll never be alone and we can always take care of each other.

"But how did you become a lost soul?"

My shadow unravels and spreads out under my feet. *I do not like to remember all that I have lost. Not when I have gained you.*

"I'm sorry. You don't have to tell me if you don't wish to."

Dar is silent for a few moments as she glides to the other side of the floor. But when she circles back, she speaks. *I—I died in a horrible accident. It was painful and sudden and cursed me to wander as a lost soul.*

"Oh Dar," I say. "Why didn't you tell me this before? If I'd known sooner, I would have done anything to help you become whole again."

My shadow shrugs. *It is asking a lot. I did not wish to be a burden. But this situation threatens us both.*

"Don't be silly. You're my best friend. What can I do?" The idea of Dar being flesh and blood, a real human girl, is utterly thrilling, despite the otherwise grave circumstances.

It is a ritual, and there is much preparation to be done. It must be performed at the height of the blood moon, a rare event that will occur during this lunar cycle. But those details can wait. First, I will take care of Tate.

"How?" I ask, suddenly curious.

Change his mind, of course. I will alter his mind completely.

I frown, a whisper of apprehension brushing over me. "You won't do anything that will hurt him, though, right?"

Of course not. I can fix everything without a single drop of blood or ounce of pain.

Dar seems to grow, gathering more shadow to her. And when I lie down in my bed and pull the covers over me, she stretches herself under the door and slinks down the hall, until all I can see is the thin line of darkness that tethers her to my feet.

CHAPTER FIVE

Screams wake me the next morning. Instinct has me reaching for Dar and gathering all the shadows in the room around me before I realize I'm not in any danger.

The screams come from the guest wing of the mansion. Fear pricks at the back of my brain. "What could have happened?" I wonder aloud, and for once, Dar has no response.

I fling off the covers and throw on my robe and slippers, then open my door. It is silent now, nary a servant in sight. Strange for the family quarters at this time of day. Curiosity carries me on light feet to the other end of the house.

An army of servants mutter and wring their hands outside the guest rooms. The ones belonging to Lord Tate.

Dread slides over my skin. Kendra notices me, then quickly drops her eyes and limps back to the wall, her pale hair falling over her face. A fear I somehow never truly saw before last night spreads through the crowd like wildfire. They draw back, some running off down the opposite corridor. All have faces twisted with the same slate of emotions: fear, suspicion. Even hate.

Dar winds around my ankles. *They are stupid. They don't know any better than to fear what they don't understand.*

That is why I need Dar. She understands, like no one ever has nor ever will. Unexpected tears brim in my eyes.

You've done no wrong. Hold your head up, and pay them no mind.

Drawing strength from my shadow, I do as she suggests, and march forward to the now unguarded door. Something must have happened to Lord Tate. "Was he all right when you left him?" I whisper to Dar.

He was perfect.

For some reason, I don't find that as comforting as I'd hoped. I step into the room to find my parents and Tate's entourage surrounding the bed. My parents say nothing upon my arrival, only giving me a stern glance. Tate's servants show me the same fear and disgust as my own. It rolls off them in hot waves. Only that strange little girl, Simone, seems oblivious to my presence. She stands by the foot of the bed, staring wide-eyed at her master.

He is terribly still. The bedclothes are so pristine that the bed hardly seems slept in. I cannot tell whether he even breathes. Last night his skin was tanned from a life spent in a sun-kissed land; today his face is as pale as the little girl's. The doctor at his bedside is saying something about a coma, a deep sleep. No one can wake him.

And then everyone looks at me.

I should have stayed in my rooms this morning.

Run, Dar says. I ignore her this time even though instinct says the same. Something tells me that would be the worst possible thing I could do right now.

"Emmeline," my father says. "What did you do?"

Shock roots me to the floor. "What? I did nothing. I was asleep in my room last night."

"This is not one of your games?" Mother says, suspicion dancing across her features.

How could they believe I would do this? "Of course not. I'd never hurt anyone."

I swallow a twinge of guilt as I think of Kendra's twisted ankle and the last guest's broken arm.

Tate's nephew Alden speaks up. "I saw what you did last night. We know you can work with shadows."

"So?" I fold my arms over my chest.

Run, Emmeline, Dar says again, with more urgency this time. But now the servants have closed the door behind me, and I can feel the hum of their presence on the other side. I wouldn't get far.

"There was a witness."

"Good, then they can tell you it wasn't me," I say. My bold words mask the uncertainty I feel inside. The witness must be one of the servants. Would they lie just to spite me? Has everyone in this house turned against me and Dar?

The man scowls. "All the witness saw was a long shadow with no one nearby to cast it. They chalked it up to a trick of the light until Lord Tate was found this morning."

Horror sinks into my skin like oil. Dar said she'd make sure I didn't have to go with Tate...and now this. But she claims

Tate was fine when she left him. She said that she was just going to change his mind and yet…

I don't know what to think anymore. All I know is Dar was the only shadow I sent into that room. If she did something, the fault is mine.

Dar perches on my shoulder and whispers in my ear. *You are not to blame, Emmeline. I told you, it is easy for them to lash out at what they do not understand.*

The man addresses my father. "She must not be allowed to harm anyone else. I have sent for the best Zinnian physicians to heal Lord Tate. But if he dies, she must return with us to Zinnia for punishment."

My father steps forward and grabs my arm, ushering me out of the room and back down the hall before I can recover my wits enough to object.

The servants do not spare me their sidelong glances as my father drags me back to my chambers.

"We have had enough, your mother and I," Father says.

"We can take no more of this behavior of yours. For years, we have protected you, even after—" He swallows hard instead of finishing his sentence, but I hear what he does not say.

"I didn't do anything to Lord Tate. I swear it," I say, but he pays me no mind. When we reach my rooms, he flings the door open and drops me unceremoniously on my bed. Dar is ruby red by now and spreads over half the floor.

My father faces me with a resigned expression. "This is too much, Emmeline. You and your shadow weaving, all the strange tricks you play. We have lost nearly all the friends we ever had since…since what happened with Rose. Our very place in society is threatened, and this was a chance to redeem ourselves. The Zinnian nobles are powerful and would have made strong allies."

I wrap my arms around my middle to stop them from shaking. I had no idea that was the case, let alone that my parents blamed me for the incident all this time. It was just an accident.

"All we asked was for you to give the cure a chance. It could have allowed all of us to have a better life." Father shakes his head. "But you couldn't do it. You couldn't just go with him and try. You had to do *this*."

"I was asleep in my rooms the whole time—"

My father holds up his hand. "Stop. Enough lies, Emmeline. The doctors aren't sure what you did, but who else could cause a shadow to enter a room without being there to cast it?"

I wish I had a good response, something—anything— with which to deny that one troubling fact. I glance at Dar, who has been strangely silent during this exchange with my father. What did she do? Did she go too far? Was this how she planned to keep me from having to go away to Zinnia? Dar is loyal to a fault, that I know. But would she do this? And if so, how? She is only a shadow.

A thousand questions tumble through my brain, but no answers follow. My father takes my hands and his expression softens.

"Emmeline, if you did something accidentally and didn't mean to, tell us what happened and the doctors might be able to fix it. You can make this right."

It's a trick, Dar whispers. *He wants you to admit to harming Lord Tate. Then they'll have to give you up to the Zinnians for punishment and be rid of you for good. Even the cure they offered before would be better than that.*

I hardly know what to think. If I tell him I sent Dar into Tate's room, I may as well be sentencing myself to be punished by the Zinnians. But if I don't, then I'm lying. A gulf yawns at my feet, and it's up to me to decide whether to leap across.

I twist my fingers together in my lap, then stare into my father's eyes and shake my head. "It wasn't me."

He straightens up and releases my hands. "I thought we raised you better than this." He leaves my room, the lock in the door clicking loudly behind him.

Even to me, my words taste like lies.

CHAPTER SIX

I sit in stunned silence on the edge of my bed, unable to fully comprehend what this means for me. Dar slides over and settles onto the ivory lace bedspread.

"Dar, what happened when you visited Tate last night?" My voice trembles.

I told you, I changed his mind. It's not my fault his mind is weak.

I stare at her, fear creeping over me like a long shadow. It has always been Dar by my side. How can I doubt my only friend?

You cannot remain here, she says, interrupting my thoughts. *You must flee.*

"I can't," I say, twisting my hands in the blanket.

Staying would be infinitely worse. Trust me, you do not want to feel the Zinnians' wrath. They are more dangerous than you know, and Lord Tate was only the tip of the iceberg.

I frown. "You know the Zinnians? But how?"

Dar turns a shade so dark she looks like a blotch of ink spilled on my bed. *I grew up in Zinnia. It is a terrible place. Oh, it is sunny, and the rolling green hills are lovely to be sure, but the people are bred with evil in their bones.*

I shudder. "What happened to you, Dar? I know you said there was an accident, but how did you become a lost soul?"

She hesitates, like she isn't sure she should tell me. *My parents were poor, and I was put to work when I was a little older than you. I was in training to be a seamstress. I loved it, making pretty things from bolts of cloth. Perhaps that's what drew me to you. Your shadow weaving reminds me of it.* Dar slides off my bed and onto the floor again. *One day a haughty young noblewoman, Lady Aisling, paid a visit to the shop.*

A lump wells in my throat. "Lady Aisling? The same woman Lord Tate works for?"

Yes, the very one.

I shudder.

Lady Aisling's visit began as usual. We took her measurements and helped her select rich fabrics and colors and bows for an array of clothing. But when my mistress told her it would be a whole week until her massive order was completed, everything fell apart.

Dar pauses and her edges redden. "What happened?" I ask, unable to contain my curiosity.

She threw a fit. Screaming and cursing at us, insisting we were the laziest dressmakers she'd ever known. All while she tore through the shop, upending boxes and throwing around anything that wasn't pinned down to the floor. The fit was so violent that it knocked an entire wall of heavy bolts of fabric down on my head. I did not survive it.

"How did your soul get lost?" I have to admit, it seems very unusual to me.

I am not entirely sure. One minute, the bolts were falling, and the next I was floating through a haze, only able to see bits and scraps of the human world. I have been wandering these lands ever since.

"I am so sorry. That is awful."

All the nobles in Zinnia are just like Lady Aisling. Haughty, selfish, and cruel. When they are angered, they're terrifying. I cannot bear the thought of you being on the receiving end of it too.

My breath catches in my throat. I know it would be foolish to run, but would it really be worse to stay? Could Dar be right?

"But I love it here. I don't want to leave my home." That is the crux of the problem. I don't want to go, which is why I agreed to the deal with Dar in the first place. So I could stay.

Dar runs her cool, shadowy fingers through my hair. *I know you do. We both do. But if you remain, the Zinnians will take you away anyway.*

A chill slithers over me. "To punish me, you mean?"

Dar shrugs. *Perhaps. Or maybe this time your parents won't ask you nicely to go with them. You've heard what they say when they don't know you're listening—they think you're crazy just like the servants do. They may force you to undergo the Zinnians' "cure." You'd never be able to mold the shadows again.*

I shudder. "I thought you said you were taking care of that."

Dar harrumphs and slides off the bed again. Try as I might, I can't shake the needling worry or the image of Lord Tate pale as death in the guest room. I lower my voice to a whisper. "Did you do this to Tate? Is that what you meant by fixing things?"

Dar puffs out. *I did what needed to be done.*

"So that's how you changed Tate's mind? You put him in a coma?" Something cold and hard begins to form in my chest, like my heart is freezing over.

I did not mean to. She deflates. *But he will live, and now, he cannot take you away.*

I swallow hard. "Can you fix it? Can you undo whatever you've done?"

I'm sorry, but I can't in this form. If I were flesh again, maybe. Dar slinks farther across the room then circles back up on the bed, almost like she's pacing.

Her unspoken words hang in the air between us: I'm the one who can bring her back to a full life.

I remember skinned knees from tripping through the woods when I was little, soothed by Dar's misty hands. Whispered words of comfort in my ears when I'd wake screaming from nightmares and no one else came to hold me. Days of lessons alone in my rooms with only Dar to help me learn my letters because the long string of tutors refused to return. I may not like the circumstances, but I know in my heart that Dar is protecting me still, in her own way, even now. And this time, I can do something for her in return. Then we'll finally be able to have a real life friendship that no one else can deny or judge.

I pull at a loose thread on the edge of my blanket. "I've never been far from home. I've never even left the grounds of this estate." After the incident, Mother and Father never wanted to take me anywhere. "Where would we go? What would we do? What if I can't carry out the ritual for you? All I'm good at is crafting shadows and scaring other people."

I'll show you how to perform the ritual, then we can come back and make everything right again. It must be done at the height of the full blood moon, and the next one is a week or so away. The timing is just right. I can help you fix things, but only if I'm made flesh. I will always take care of you, Emmeline. Leave tonight, and you can be free. She pauses. *We both can.*

I look away and out the window instead. The sun glares in, making me blink. What will I have to do to perform the ritual that will set her free?

"I don't know if I can do this." It was one thing when I agreed to let Dar change Lord Tate's mind. It's another to throw myself to the wilds and rely on her for survival. Here at home, we are never without a cook.

Sensing my uneasiness, Dar wraps around my shoulders. *You will make it through this. We will do it together.*

"But will Lord Tate?" I say before I can think better of it. Fighting with Dar isn't going to help me.

He will, once you set me free. But he might not if you stay here. The soldiers from Zinnia are already on their way. They sent their fastest sparrow with a message as soon as Tate was discovered.

"How do you know?"

Because I know the Zinnians. If they deem you guilty, they will throw you in a cell—a well-lit one with no shadows just for you—and let you rot until they decide to cure you. What will become of me then? Please, save yourself. Save us both.

I can sense the desperation in her plea. She knew the Zinnians in her first life. She knows what we'd be getting into, and she needs me to get us both out of it.

Flee, and we'll be free.

My head pounds with confusion and fear, but a sudden clarity fills me. "You're right. We'll leave at dusk."

By the time dusk falls, a small platoon of men with silver helmets and bright green cloaks appears in the yard bathed in the first shadows of the evening.

My insides upend themselves. Dar was right.

My family will not come to my aid; they'll send me away with the Zinnians, and I'll never be the same again. I might even become like that horrible little girl, Simone. Fear tightens my chest, making it difficult to breathe.

We must hurry, Dar warns.

Unfortunately, my door is still locked despite my best efforts to pick it this afternoon. I gather all the shadows in the room and begin forming a length of rope. Silently, I open the window and fasten my shadow rope to the foot of my bed. Then I slowly lower it down the side of the house. No doubt some of the soldiers are inside, but the ones who remain mill around between a handful of tents on our back lawn. I'll have to get by them to reach the forest. I can use the shadows to my advantage there.

But first, I need food. There's no way I can survive on my own for even a day if I don't find my way to the kitchens first. I lower myself down, nervous only for a moment. I've never used shadows to carry my weight before, and I'm relieved when it holds. I shimmy down the rope and land in the shadow of one of the small bushes that dots the yard. The bone-white brick wall of the house rises up at my back. I crouch, Dar at my side, and pull the shadows in the rope around me to form a blanket. I creep along the side of the mansion, sticking as close to it as possible, until I reach the servants' entrance to the kitchens.

I slip inside, holding my breath once the door closes behind us. I count to ten, just to be safe. No shouts arise, and no servants have spied me here. It's dinnertime, and the cook and the servants must be busy bringing the food into the dining hall. Probably busier than usual with the additional guests.

If it's time for dinner, they'll discover you're gone soon, Dar says.

Drat, she's right. They'll bring my dinner to my rooms. And I won't be there to answer the knock at my door. The alarm could go up any second.

I duck into the kitchen and grab an empty flour sack discarded nearby. I fill it as heavy as I can stand with fruit and bread and jerky. I even swipe a couple of my favorite tarts.

Don't forget water, Dar reminds me as I'm about to leave.

I hunt for a moment, then find a water skein in a cupboard. I toss it in the flour sack too, then throw that over my shoulder. I wish I had a real pack, but I've never needed one before. This will have to do.

We sneak back outside, and I cautiously make my way to the side of the house facing the woods. The lawn feels like an enormous expanse with the tents and the guards standing between me and the trees. I duck down behind a shrub and call my shadows to me.

Then I begin to weave. The shadows, responding to my call, thread together to create the shapes I envision in my mind. One twist of my wrist, and they move into position like my own personal army waiting for a command.

As far as the soldiers standing guard can see, it is only one shadow that moves at first, maybe cast by a tree in the night breeze. Then another wiggles at the edge of the yard, startling the nearest soldier. Yet another moves like a rustling shrub where no shrub really is. The guard cries out, and steps forward to investigate.

My murmuring shadows surround the makeshift camp.

The soldiers exchange wary, wide-eyed glances but can't find a cause. No one notices one more shadow dodging across the lawn, not when the shadow blanket I've made blends so perfectly with the darkness.

Breathless, I make it to the tree line and take one last, lingering look at my home. Then I step into the forest, and the shadows swallow me whole.

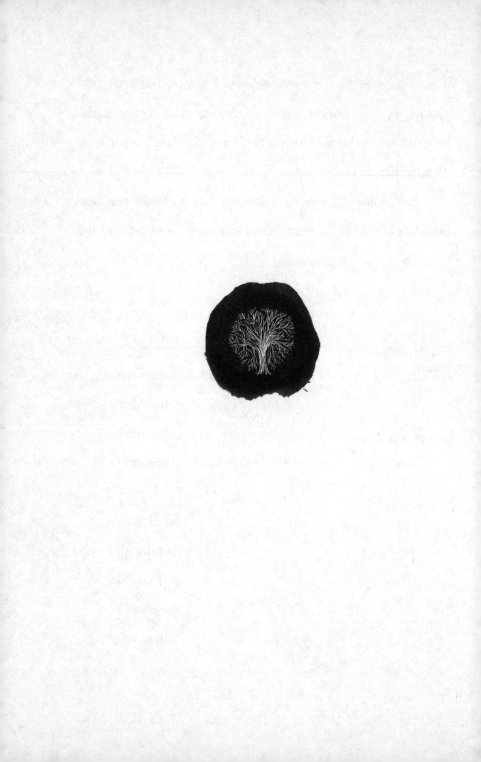

CHAPTER SEVEN

e flee through the woods and darkness, and the tall trees form a cocoon around us in welcome. Dar clings to me, hiding me from anything else that may be haunting the woods after dusk.

When the cry finally goes up that I'm missing, all we hear are distant echoes.

They have horses and may catch up if we stop, Dar says.

I shudder. I don't like horses. Or rather, they don't like me. The one time I ventured into the stables when I was younger, our mare and stallion reared and frothed at the mouth. I was spirited away, though whether it was for my safety or theirs I could not say.

Mother said my magic scared them. They could smell it on me, just the same as fear or an apple concealed in a pocket.

We keep moving, the trees' shadows lengthening and curling around me. Far away, the sounds of hooves and branches snapping trickle toward us, spurring me to move faster.

We'll outpace them. I know it.

I can't explain why Dar is so sure of this, but I have no choice but to trust her. It isn't long before my breath becomes ragged and my legs begin to ache. "I can't do it. I have to stop."

Just a little farther. There's a break in the trees ahead.

I grumble but pick up my feet, one after the other. Regret fills my lungs. Fleeing is not particularly fun, and I can't help but wish that I was at home, safe in my room.

Up ahead, moonlight breaks through the edge of the forest. But when I reach the last tree, I halt, wrapping an arm around the dark trunk, gasping.

A huge crack in the earth lies before us. A gorge. There is no bridge in sight. We have traveled considerably farther than I have ever dared to venture before.

"We're trapped," I whisper.

I can feel the weight of Dar's smile at my back. *Hardly. This is perfect. If they follow, they'll have to go around for who knows how many miles to find a bridge.*

A hint of excitement warms my cheeks. "But I can make my own. The shadow rope held my weight. A shadow bridge should too."

It will, trust me.

Sneaking down one story of a building using a shadow rope is one thing; walking out onto open air and a who-knows-how-deep drop is another entirely. The hoofbeats in the distance pound in my ears, and my hands suddenly turn slick.

I have no other choice.

My magic takes hold of the nearest shadows cast by the tall trees, laying them across the gorge like long flat boards. They hit the edge of the other side and stick in place, just as I direct. Soon more shadow boards join, and twining smoky ropes lash the boards together and secure themselves around trees on either side to form a railing.

The sounds of pursuit grow louder. A bitter taste lingers in my mouth as I eye my work.

We go together, Dar says.

I swallow my fear and set one foot on the shadow plank bridge. It holds my weight. Then my other foot. My hands squeeze the shadow railing. Dizziness, part from exhilaration, part from terror, swims across my vision.

One foot after the other. Look straight ahead.

Halfway across the gorge, echoing voices reach my ears, joining the hoofbeats. My heart stammers in my chest.

Go! Dar urges, but I make the mistake of glancing down.

Every limb turns to stone. The drop is impossible. Water rushes far below over rocks and fallen logs, a frothy, sparkling ribbon in the moonlight.

Dar screams in my ears. *Emmeline! They're coming!*

I close my eyes to shut out the drop and steady my throbbing pulse. Then I run headlong the rest of the way across the bridge. I stumble into the grass on the other side and fall to my knees.

The hoofbeats grow louder, mingling with the braying of the horses. With a wave of my hand, I send the pieces of my shadow bridge scattering back to their proper places in the night.

"Thank you," I whisper to the departing shadows as I run

for the cover of the forest on this side of the gorge. I hide behind one of the trees to catch my breath. The pounding hoofbeats reach a fever pitch then halt suddenly. Dar and I curl around our tree to see if our pursuers realize where I've gone.

There are so many, Dar says.

Indeed, there are. The green cloaks of the guards stand out in the night, moving in a rhythm known only to their circling horses.

Look! Dar laughs. *The gorge has perplexed them. They're returning to the forest!*

It is a welcome sight to see them maneuver their horses farther down the edge of the gorge. A weight lifts from my chest, but I squash the laugh that bubbles inside for fear of giving myself away.

"They must think they passed us."

Then we're safe for now. Dar wraps around my shoulders, and I lean into the familiar comfort. *We should go a little farther. Then you can stop to rest.*

I press on through the trees. The moon is high above our heads, and my beloved fireflies flicker around us like stars come down from the heavens. If I wasn't exhausted, I'd be twirling through the ferns that coat the forest floor. But here there is no path for us to follow, and no way of knowing what lies ahead. Just the thought makes me feel weightless and lost.

When we reach an outcropping of boulders made from a deep-black stone, I finally stop. My feet will take me no farther tonight. I wrap the shadows around me, and lay down on a bed of pine needles between the rocks.

"Dar, what did you look like when you were alive?"

I hardly remember. I was a shape shifter, so I was rarely in my original form anyway. And it was so long ago that I don't recall. I lost so much to the Zinnians.

I wonder how old she was, what color hair and eyes she had. Was she pretty and admired? How many people mourned her loss?

I suppose we shall find out, Dar says. *Once you perform the ritual and bring me back.*

A smile dances over my lips. This is the one happy thing about my flight from home: Dar will soon be real. My best friend will be flesh and blood and can fully join in with our games.

"I can't wait," I say.

I begin to drift off, and Dar tucks herself under my head like a pillow, whispering stories in my ear until I fall asleep.

———•———

When the light of a new day wakes me, I ache all over. I've never had to run that far that quickly in my whole life. The pain in my limbs is joined by a fierce tightness in my chest.

I have no idea where we are. We are far from my parents' estate and the trees I've befriended. There are pines and oaks, but some trees have strange white bark and others a deep reddish purple. I know the ferns, but many more plants grow here that I cannot name. Nothing is familiar. I never even knew that ravine we traversed last night existed.

Frustration and tears well up as I poke through the flour sack of provisions I brought with me. I am terribly thirsty, and I drain the water skein immediately even though Dar warns me not to. I take a bite of one of the pastries I brought. The crust is flaky and sweet, and it makes me miss home more than anything has since I left. Life was simple and easy there. I didn't have to worry about things like water and food. I could play with my shadows, unconcerned with necessities.

I wonder if the shadows in the woods and the corners of the mansion miss me as much as I miss them?

We should set out, Dar says.

"I need to find more water first." The ground past the boulders slopes downward. Perhaps farther along it meets the river we saw far below the shadow bridge last night.

You should have drunk it sparingly, she says, her shape spreading over the ground near me.

"I will drink what I want," I snap, then get to my feet. I shouldn't be short with her, but there's no help for it now.

Dar goes silent, and her coloring is lighter than usual. A trick of the sun? Or is she mad at me too?

"We'll have to find the river that runs through that gorge. We don't have a destination in mind; what does a little detour matter?"

My shadow has nothing to say to this, but her shape has grown smaller, like she doesn't even want to touch me right now. Something in the pit of my stomach twists.

I gather my things, then straighten my spine and march in

the direction I believe the river went. My aching muscles object with every step. If I walk far enough, I'll have to hit water of some kind eventually. I hope.

As far as I can tell, we are still within the domain of my family's territory, Parilla. According to my books, there should be several villages scattered between their estate and the border with the next territory over, Abbacho. Zinnia is on the opposite side of Parilla. In other words, every step ought to take me farther beyond their reach.

The boulders I slept between last night were at the top of a steep hill. The journey down is not as easy as I'd hoped. In many places the incline is sharp, and I have to walk around for who knows how far to find an easier slope. The trees here don't seem to be troubled by it at all. Instead, they grow out from the side of the hill, giving the landscape the appearance of being some sort of many-armed beast.

The sun moves across the sky, and my thirst grows stronger along with an ache in my stomach. I hate to admit it but Dar is right. I should have drunk the water more slowly. She still hasn't said a word and trails a few feet behind me on a thin shadow string like a wayward balloon.

It's rather lonely out here in the woods with no one to talk to.

But the birds chirp freely, and strange small creatures tumble through the undergrowth. Velvet ferns cover the hillside, nearly as high as my waist, and I run my hands over the tops as I pass through them.

Suddenly another sound joins them. Something loud and thunderous, but it began so gradually that I'm almost upon whatever makes the sound before I understand what I'm hearing.

I hit another steep incline, but the view gives me hope. Below it runs a river that's strong and clear. Just the sight of it makes my dry mouth water with need.

I can create many things from shadows, but no amount of wishing will allow me to create real, drinkable water from it.

The shadows of the nearby trees heed my call eagerly, the smaller ones cast by the thinning ferns, and any others creeping down the hill. I spool them together, creating a circular shape in the air. Thinning it out, I make it wider and curved like a shallow bowl. When I'm finished, I choose a launch point with the least amount of trees between me and the riverbank. I place my shadow sled on the ground as close as

I dare to where the incline sharpens and settle inside it, tying my flour sack to my belt.

Then I shove off. At first, the slide down the hill is exhilarating with the wind rushing through my hair.

"Dar! Look how fast we're going!" She doesn't answer, still sulking behind me.

But when the shadow sled hits a rock and sends me careening into the path of a large tree, panic slides up my insides. Desperately I try to guide the sled away, but it sends me spinning instead.

Without warning, I'm hurled into the air.

Brief glimpses of the underbellies of ferns and crunching sticks and leaves are all I see as I tumble head over heels the rest of the way down the hill. I land on the grassy riverbank and manage to grab hold of a sapling's trunk before I'm tossed into the water.

Something whistles over my head, and I duck. Breathlessly, I gape as my sled hits the water and the shadows disintegrate into the waves.

My stomach drops into my shoes. That might have been me had I not been thrown off first.

The river roils around rocks that jut out from the water, spitting foam onto the bank. The grass here is green and cool, but that is the only thing calm about where I've landed.

"Dar?" I say in a small voice, hugging my arms around my knees. "Please talk to me. I need you. Don't leave me alone."

Shadow arms curl around my trembling form. *It's all right. You're safe. Best not to try that again, I think.*

A strangled laugh escapes my throat. "No, I don't think I will." I sigh. "But I do need more water." I'm rather proud that I managed to keep my flour sack the whole way down. I don't know what I'd do if I lost my food.

I swallow the sand in my throat and pull out the water skein. I am only a few feet from the river's edge, but it's a roaring, churning thing. The most water I've ever seen at once is a pond out in the woods of my family's estate, and that was as placid as a pane of glass.

Every muscle tenses as I step closer, eying the rocks in the water warily.

Be careful and stay low, Dar advises. *There's a tree a little ways down near the water. You can hold on to that to brace yourself.*

Relief begins to dull the needling fear. "Thank you," I say. I missed Dar while she wasn't speaking to me.

I do as my shadow instructs, grasping the tree with one arm and reaching into the water with the other. When the skein is full, I skitter away from the edge, gulping water in so quickly my stomach begins to heave.

Don't drink too fast! Dar says. *You'll make yourself sick.*

I choke the water down, but this time I listen to her and drink more slowly. Then I repeat the process to refill the skein. I'll need it again later, and I'm not keen on braving a hill like that a second time.

"Where should we go?" I ask, pulling leaves from my hair. My dress is now caked in grass and mud from the wet dirt near the river. I can feel the hot blush of bruises forming on my limbs and the sting from scrapes scattered over my skin, but otherwise, I am unhurt.

I ought to get back on my feet, but after all the walking I did this morning, it's nice to sit here on the riverbank for a few moments.

Anywhere we want.

I frown at her form, now billowing in the breeze like

the drawings I've seen of sails on ships. "But surely you had a destination in mind. Where must we go to get what we need to perform the ritual that will bring you fully back to life?"

There is no one place we need to be, except away from Zinnia and those guards. My shadow's edges glow red. Even the thought of Zinnia is enough to upset her.

"But what do I have to do?" I ask.

All in good time. We should get farther away first. Just to be safe.

I can't deny the sensibility in that. For all we know the guards are still running rampant through these woods. I'm sure they must have found a way across the gorge by now. In fact, they could be anywhere.

A sickly sensation crawls across my skin, like I'm being watched. I seal the water skein and toss it in my sack.

"Let's go," I say. Dar shivers, though whether it's with fear of the soldiers or the excitement of her wish getting nearer to fulfillment, I cannot tell. We're exposed on the bank of the river, and we stick close to the side of the hill and the cover of trees as much as possible. I use my shadowcraft to stretch the shadow of each tree as far as I can toward the next to lend us more cover.

We make our way slowly, but steadily, creeping toward the safety of deeper forest. I only hope what waits there is not worse.

CHAPTER EIGHT

We don't encounter the Zinnian soldiers again until midafternoon. We stop to rest under the shade of an enormous gnarled oak tree when the sounds of metal armor clanking and hooves striking the forest floor send me scurrying into the branches of the tree. I climb as high as I dare, then huddle close to the trunk, wrapping the great tree's shadow around me like a blanket.

I hold my breath as the sounds get closer, hammering into my head. Soon their green cloaks come into view. One of them pauses not far from the tree and dismounts his horse, sending my pulse flying. He bends over and picks up something in the leaves.

The apple core I tossed away mere minutes before we heard them. I was so startled I didn't even think of it. Dar tenses behind me, her form reddening. This time I don't dare to move and smooth the edges of her shape to calm her like I usually do.

"Someone was here, and not long ago either," says the guard. The man on the lead horse circles back, turning to his men. I'm startled to realize I recognize him as Tate's nephew, Alden.

"Hurry, the girl can't be far now." Alden turns his horse, and he and the rest of the guards trot away from where I hide in the tree.

My breath releases from my body, and I slump against the trunk. My knees feel as weak as blades of grass.

"That was much too close," I whisper to Dar.

We have the advantage now. They're ahead of us. We know which way not to go.

"Thank goodness for that."

I let a few more moments go by, not yet ready to risk the climb down with my hands still quivering. It is peaceful up here, and I can see an empty birds' nest from where I sit. Did I frighten them, or was it the guards?

Finally, I clamber down, scraping my arms on the way.

The ground under my feet is a welcome relief. But from my hiding spot in the shadow of the great tree, a pleasing sound captures my attention.

A voice singing somewhere in these woods.

I peer around the tree. Up ahead, in the opposite direction from the path the guards took, the light seems to have grown brighter, as though the sun just decided to say hello and shined itself up for the day.

The music comes from the same direction. Something about it is familiar, and it draws me in.

After quickly checking that no wayward soldiers follow the others who passed moments ago, I hurry to the next tree. But it isn't close enough. I must hear the music better. See for myself who or what is making it.

I dodge from tree to tree up the hill, always careful to keep the shadows wrapped around me. Through the trees, I spy the edge of a field and flowers shining like gold in the afternoon light.

Where are you going, Emmeline? Dar asks, a hint of irritation in her voice, but I ignore her for once. The pull of the music and light is too strong to resist.

I pause by a tree at the edge of the field. Crouching close to the ground, I peer around the tree trunk and choke on my gasp.

In the center of the field stands the source of the music—and the light: a boy, not much older than me, surrounded by knee-high strands of grass and white and yellow flowers that look like lace. His mouth is open and the melody that drew me here flows from it. Light swirls around his body, painting him in every possible shade of yellow and gold. The light isn't just growing brighter, it's moving in sparkling bands, circling his frame in time to the music. It forms a perfect orb around him. There is something else in the air too. Something fizzy. Something I recognize.

My breath stutters.

He is using light in much the same way I use shadows. He has magic.

I have never met anyone else with a talent before.

My feet take me closer to the field.

It could be a trap! Dar hisses in my ear.

"No, I'm sure it's not," I say breathlessly. "He's…he's using magic. I recognize the way it feels."

Dar doesn't say another word when I step into the field. The bands of light have expanded around the boy, his circle close enough that I could reach out and touch the gilded edges.

"Isn't it beautiful, Dar?" I whisper, but she makes no response.

I pause, debating whether to take another step. The boy hasn't seen me yet, but I can't help wanting to know his name. To know what he calls his delightful sort of magic. Dar will be angry, but I can't quell the sudden longing to know someone else who might understand me. Who might understand what it's like to have magic and all that entails. And to actually talk to them, not just observe as I usually do.

My decision is inevitable. I step farther into the field, letting the boy's music and light wrap around me like the warmth of a blazing fire. I glance down at my feet and the sight steals my breath away.

My shadow has vanished. Her voice, my constant comfort, is silent. In fact, the field is so full of brilliant light that it is completely devoid of shadows. A chill prickles over my arms, but my feet do not falter.

I am halfway across the field when he sees me. His voice cuts off, and the music and light vanish.

I halt, frozen in his gaze. How silly must I appear, with a flour sack over my shoulder, gaping at him.

He pales and takes a step back.

"Hello?" I call. "I'm sorry, I just—I heard you singing, and it was lovely."

The boy glances around warily, and I realize his hair and skin isn't as golden as they first appeared. It was an effect of the light. His skin is pale, and his hair is a dirty blond. His eyes are the brightest green I've ever seen in my life.

"I just wanted to say hello." My hands fiddle with the flour sack, wishing I had a better explanation to offer.

The boy relaxes a little. "It's all right. You just surprised me. I never see anyone this deep into the hills."

I frown. "What are you doing all the way out here, anyway? Is a village nearby?"

"I could ask the same of you." He shakes his head and walks a little closer. "I don't live in a village. I live here."

"In the woods?"

"Yes."

We move toward each other in a halting dance, a few steps for him, a few for me, until mere feet separate us. "All alone?" I ask.

He laughs, and it reminds me of his song, sharp and clear. "My parents have a cottage nearby." He snaps his mouth shut, as if he regrets his words.

"Sorry, I didn't mean to pry. You have a wonderful voice."

Red blotches form on his cheeks, and he glances down at his feet. "Thanks." He scuffs a toe against a wayward rock. "What are you doing out here?"

It is my turn to hedge.

Lie, Dar insists, back at my side so suddenly that I wonder if I just imagined she had vanished. *You must lie to him. It is the only way to remain safe. We know no one outside the estate, and we must be cautious.*

The thought of lying to the first person I've ever met who has a talent turns my stomach, but it is more sensible than telling everyone what I am. Especially when the guards are still out there hunting me. Now that I've come to see what people really think of my shadowcraft, I must know him a little better first. I don't know that I could bear yet another person being frightened of me just because of my shadow weaving. Or worse, thinking I'm crazy because I talk to my shadow too.

"I—I worked at an estate east of here. My mistress was cruel and…and I suppose I'm hiding from her. At least until I can find another household," I say, surprised at how easily the lie rolls off my tongue.

The boy considers me quietly for a moment.

Show him your bruises, Dar whispers. *That ought to convince him.*

I was so taken with this boy's light magic that I almost forgot about my adventure this morning that left my legs and arms scattered with cuts and bruises. They have ached the whole way here.

"She wasn't a kind mistress." I roll up my sleeves, unable to meet the boy's eyes. There are more cuts than I recall, and they sting as the fabric brushes over them. He sucks his breath in sharply, and his expression softens.

"You need to clean those scrapes," he says. "And a poultice would help with the bruises." He gives me one more long look before holding out his hand across the space between us. "I'm Lucas."

I take his hand and shake it. "Emmeline."

"If you want, I can bring you to my house, and my mother can patch you up."

I smile. "Thank you, that's very kind."

I follow him, and Dar sighs, but I can't ask her why without attracting attention. He leads me into the woods on the other side of the field and onto a path half-hidden by the undergrowth. I am dying to ask him about his magic, but given his reaction to being caught using it, I fear that might shatter the fragile trust we've forged. I decide to wait until we've known each other for more than a few fleeting moments.

"We don't see many people out here," Lucas says. "Travelers sometimes but never people my age and definitely never alone."

"Are you sure your parents won't mind you bringing me into your home?"

He shakes his head, and the sunlight tangles in his hair. "Mum will love having a girl in the house." He grins over his shoulder. "I think sometimes she gets a bit tired of just me and Pa hanging around."

I laugh unexpectedly. It is difficult for me to fathom any mother being happy to have me in her house.

The trees break ahead to reveal a clearing. At the center is a quaint cottage painted white with green shutters. In the front yard is a little garden of wildflowers and along the side, a huge vegetable patch. A little barn peeks out from behind the vegetable patch. It is simple and lovely and everything my own home was not.

"Are you coming?" Lucas frowns at me from a few feet away, and only then do I realize that I have stopped.

"Yes, of course." I hurry after him, and he leads me up the walk and right through his front door. My heart jumps into my throat for a brief moment, as my imagination half expects the guards to be lying in wait for me here. But there is only a gaily painted interior flooded with the warm, welcoming smells of vegetable soup and baking bread. I pause to breathe it in, and that warmth fills me too.

Be careful, Dar warns. I open my eyes and find Lucas staring at me again.

I cover my foolishness with a smile. "It smells wonderful here!"

He breaks into a grin. "That's my mum. She's the best cook. And she's pretty handy with poultices and bandages too."

He gestures to my arms. "I should know; she uses them on me often enough."

"Lucas?" a woman's voice calls from the kitchen. "Who are you talking to—" His mother appears in the doorway and stops short. Her hair is dark, and pieces float around her head, escaping the braid she's pulled it into. "Lucas, who is this?" Her voice is careful and studied, like she has an inherent mistrust of strangers. Her keen dark eyes narrow, but nothing can hide their warmth.

"Mum, this is Emmeline. I met her in the woods. She was a servant, but her mistress used her ill. She's off to find a new household."

His mother crosses her arms over her chest. "She's a runaway?"

Careful, Dar says. *Too many people haven't appreciated you and your talent. She might try to send you back where you came from.*

My heart speeds up. That would be disastrous. We've come too far for it to all be for nothing.

"I don't wish to impose. I'll just be on my way…" Before I can move to go, Lucas grabs my hand and holds out my arm.

"Mum, she needs our help. Show her, Emmeline."

I duck my head and pull up my sleeve, feeling a twinge of

87

guilt at the deception. Lies, however well-intentioned, do not sit well with me.

His mother's face softens when she sees the cuts and bruises lining my arms. "Well, that just won't do. Those fancy folk have no right to treat others like that. You can call me Miranda. Come on." She puts an arm around my shoulder and leads me into the kitchen. I shiver at the touch. I have faint memories of my mother embracing me when I was little, but it has been so long. The only one to hug me recently is Dar, and Miranda's touch is much more solid.

She brings me into the kitchen, Lucas trailing after us, and sits me down in a chair by the table. Dar is directly under my feet, and I can tell she is brimming with worry.

Be very careful, Emmeline, Dar warns. *These people are not like you and me. You'll need to be more careful about how you talk and act if you want them to believe you're really a servant.*

My pulse skitters. I hadn't even thought of that.

"Roll up your sleeves, dear," Miranda says, then begins to put herbs into a mortar and pestle. "Lucas, go get some fresh clean water, please."

He flashes a quick grin at me, then dashes off to do her

bidding. I watch his mother mash the herbs, then transfer them to a bowl and mix them with clay and salt and a few other substances I cannot name. She takes a kettle off the stove, pours a bit of hot water over the mixture, and stirs. Then she lays out a folded cloth and spoons the concoction into it. By the time Lucas reappears, she is wrapping it up.

"Put some in a clean bowl, please," she says. Lucas does and sets the bowl on the table next to me. "Now, Emmeline, hold this over each bruise for a few minutes at a time while I clean up these cuts." She *tsks*. "It's a good thing Lucas found you. With all this dirt, you're well on your way to an infection."

I swallow hard. Infection? Getting hurt, sick, or infected never even occurred to me when I undertook this journey last night.

Dar pools around my legs and squeezes my ankle. *I would have kept you safe too.*

I'll have to reassure her later, but for now, I welcome the help from Lucas and Miranda. Vague memories of skinned knees when I was little come back to me sometimes, but I can't recall anyone ever taking such care of me except for Dar. And I'm only a stranger in Miranda's home. Something wells up in my chest, making my eyes burn, but I blink it back.

Miranda tends to my cuts, and I move the poultice around my arms and legs when she instructs. When she is finished, I have to admit I feel much better. Even the bruises are beginning to ache less. She stands up, sets her bowl aside, and puts her hands on her hips.

"Now, young lady, where are your parents?"

Heat flashes over my body.

Lie! Dar insists, spilling over the kitchen floor like creeping mud. *Or she will definitely send you back. Tell her you haven't seen them in ages.*

"I haven't seen them in a long time," I say carefully. It's somewhat true. It's been almost a day, and it certainly does feel like a long time to me.

Miranda sighs. "They sold you into labor, didn't they?" She scoffs. "What kind of parents would send their child away just for a bit of peace and a handful of coins?" She settles into the chair opposite me, her eyes glancing toward her son who has been quiet but eager to help this whole time.

"Do you know where you're going?"

This time I don't have to lie. I shake my head. "No. Just away."

"Are they looking for you?"

My heart leaps into my throat, but I don't see a threat in her expression, only sympathy.

"Probably, yes."

"Well then, you may stay with us for a few days if you'd like. You'll have food and a bed, and I can keep an eye on those cuts and bruises for you. You will have to help with chores though."

"Mum!" Lucas objects.

She gives him an amused look. "No one gets out of that. We all have to pull our weight. Don't worry; it won't be much. You can help me in the garden. It could use a good weeding."

"Th-thank you," I say. "I'm happy to earn my keep."

"It's settled then. Lucas, set the table. Your father will be home for dinner soon."

I help Lucas set out the place settings while he chats and laughs with his mother. When his father, Alfred, returns home, we sit to eat, though I'm so nervous about accidentally giving myself away I hardly touch my food. Their place settings are very different from home; they only have one fork and one spoon, not the several I'm accustomed to. There may be many more differences than I thought between me and these people.

I told you, Dar whispers in my ear. *They are not like us. They seem nice, but we must be ever on our guard. You must take care to conceal that you are not who you say you are.*

The pit of my stomach sinks. When I first saw Lucas, I had so hoped he would accept me. But Dar is right. Until I know them better, they cannot know who and what I am.

Over dinner, Miranda brings her husband up to speed on why I am here. He turns his green eyes to me, pushing his glasses up the bridge of his nose, and then he swerves his gaze to Lucas.

"Where were you when you found Emmeline?"

Lucas squirms, so I offer an answer instead. "I actually found him, sir. In a field."

Alfred's face clouds over. "Lucas, what were you doing in that field?" he says quietly.

Lucas stares at his soup bowl. "Practicing," he mumbles.

"Lucas!" Miranda says, setting her napkin down. Uneasiness hovers over the table like a cloud, but I am not sure why. I fear I should not have spoken at all.

"She only saw a little bit. But Emmeline is trustworthy, I promise. She won't tell anybody, will you?"

His talent. That's what they're upset about. I know some

people are secretive about their gifts, but it hadn't occurred to me it might be to such an extent for someone like Lucas. I am only hiding mine since it has made others afraid of me, but I suppose it is not surprising that Lucas's parents would rather others not know of his talent as well.

"I won't tell a soul that you've been blessed by the Cerelia Comet, I swear," I say. My own secret dances on my lips, but I remember Dar's warning: everyone seems to fear my talent. I don't want to scare them away already.

Whatever you do, you must not tell them about me. We don't want to give them any reason to mistrust you.

Dar makes a good point. We will wait until we know more about them. Until we both believe they're trustworthy enough to confide in them.

Miranda and Alfred sigh. "I suppose there's no help for it now," Alfred says, glancing at me. "I hope you are as true to your word as Lucas says."

"Your secrets are not mine to share."

With that, Alfred takes another helping, and Lucas smiles shyly at me over his bowl. The conversation turns to livelier subjects, and soon laughter fills the room.

This family with their clear and easy affection have welcomed me into their home. I gulp down an unexpected sob. This is more kindness than I've seen in a very long time. I didn't realize how much I was missing until now.

But worry eats away at me. If they knew what I could do, would they fear me too, or would they be just as kind because of Lucas's talent? I want to share my magic with Lucas, but until I know this family better, I'll have to keep my own secrets close.

CHAPTER NINE

I wake the next morning in a borrowed bed and a borrowed nightgown. Dar and I were in such a hurry to leave that it never even occurred to me to pack a change of clothes. Lucas's mother is a small woman but still much taller than me, so the nightgown is large, as is the plain, sturdy green dress she's laid out on the chair. It is kind of her to lend them to me.

I put on the dress and tie the simple sash around my waist in such a way that it helps to conceal the fact that it hangs off my frame.

You're finally awake, Dar says, slithering across the floor. *You've slept like the dead this morning.*

"Sorry, I was exhausted. I hope we finally lost those soldiers." I yawn. I do feel more tired than usual today.

I'm dying to get out of this house. The woods call to me so keenly.

"We might need to stay indoors longer than I'd like, just to be safe." I glance at the door of the guest room. "We'll have to see what Lucas and his family do with their days. I'll need to earn my keep if we want to remain here for a while."

Nerves tremble in my limbs. I'm intrigued by this strange little family living out in the woods…and by Lucas's light magic. I hope we can stay, just until Dar and I complete that ritual.

After pulling on my boots, I go in search of signs of life. A wonderful, rich smell accompanied by laughter emanates from the kitchen. When I stand in the doorway, I see the source of the aroma that is making my mouth water: croissants, perfectly golden brown, thanks to Lucas's light singing.

He stands on his chair, music pouring from his mouth and sweeping the rays of morning light that stream through the windows into a focused beam. He bends the beam, making it circle right over the plate of croissants.

"Emmeline, have a seat, please. Lucas is almost done," Miranda says.

Lucas winks at me, and finishes his song, then sits back down on his chair, snatching a piping hot croissant in the process.

It isn't polite to gape like that, Emmeline, Dar murmurs in my ear. I snap my mouth shut. *And maybe don't sit up so straight in your chair.*

I try to hunch over a bit, but it feels awkward. My whole life, it has been driven into me to sit up straight, keep my hands folded neatly in my lap, and not talk about my shadow.

Lucas's father chuckles and takes a roll for himself. "It's all right. Lucas is an excellent baker, though his methods are a bit unusual."

"I've been practicing a lot," Lucas says.

"Yes," Miranda says. "He makes croissants at least once a week, sometimes twice if we're lucky."

"It's all about the morning light." Lucas chews thoughtfully. "Croissants need the right type of light, something gentle, but still hot enough to toast. I can never bake at noon. Everything will burn if I do."

"I had no idea light was so finicky," I say. My own shadows deepen and ebb throughout the day, so I suppose it makes sense that beams of light would have nuances too. I breathe in the wonderful smell, and my hands can't help themselves—they grab a croissant too. It is flaky, golden perfection. "This is amazing."

Lucas grins and ducks his head. "I've been thinking I might want to become a baker when I'm older. I bet I'd be the fastest cook in the region."

Alfred laughs and puts a hand on his son's shoulder. "Get through your homeschooling first; then we'll talk about careers."

I glance at Miranda. "Thank you for letting me stay here with you for a short while. What can I do to help out?"

Worry wriggles in my veins, but I do my best to ignore it. I never did a single chore at home, but I can't risk them discovering who I really am. Not yet. And if that means doing some chores, I'll make that sacrifice. I only hope I don't bungle them too horribly and give myself away.

"Can Emmeline help me bring water up from the river today?" Lucas asks.

Miranda considers. "Yes, I suppose that will do for this morning. Do you know anything about plants?"

I shake my head, not wanting to speak with my mouth full of food. Mother always told me that was a rude thing to do, and I do not wish to offend Miranda. Though perhaps it won't matter here? I no longer know where the line is, and that is very confusing.

She shrugs. "That's all right. We'll teach you. We grow most of what we eat, but we buy grain and meat when we visit the local village each week to sell our surplus. You can come with us tomorrow for that. And perhaps we can order a new dress to wear that will be a little more comfortable for you."

My cheeks flame. I really should have thought to bring clothes. I fear I am even more unprepared for this task than I realized.

"I'd love to learn about gardening," I say. If we remain on the run for long, knowing how to grow things would certainly come in handy.

Once the dishes are cleared away, Lucas leads me outside.

I close my eyes and let the sun settle on my skin, considering it in a way I haven't before. Lucas is right; the morning sun is a little gentler than noon or later in the day. I've always been so focused on my shadows that I never really noticed it before.

As a grin creeps over my face, Lucas laughs a few feet away. "What are you doing, Emmeline?"

My eyes open and I laugh too. "I was testing the light. You're right; it is gentler."

"You shouldn't be surprised. I know lots about light."

Dar harrumphs at my feet. *Shadows are still better.* I smile but don't dare to answer her here.

He leads me to a shed behind the cottage, and I follow him. The shed contains many strange instruments, including pairs of buckets suspended by ropes tied to poles. Lucas picks one and rests the pole over his shoulders, letting the buckets hang down at his sides. I frown at him.

"What's that?"

He regards me curiously. "Haven't you ever seen water buckets before?"

"Not like that. We had a well on my estate." I bite my tongue realizing I should not have called the estate mine, but thankfully Lucas doesn't seem to notice.

"Well, it's pretty easy. Just lift them by the pole and put the pole on your shoulders. Be careful the buckets don't get caught on any wayward branches once they're full. Then we'd have to go all the way back to the river."

His eyes sparkle, and I shift my gaze away quickly. His

face is full of trust and simple joys, as if he exudes sunshine from his pores. I pick up one of the pole-and-bucket contraptions. It is easier to maneuver than I expected.

"The river is this way. Mum always tells me to be extra careful when we go this far from the cottage. Be as quiet as you can be, and don't talk to strangers." He glances back at me, his dark lashes casting shadows on his cheeks. "But I guess I broke that rule with you. So, I suppose not all strangers are bad."

I laugh. "Maybe just strange adults."

"Definitely."

The woods here are lovely, and while Lucas and I trek down the slim pathway to the river, Dar ducks and dives and plays with the forest shadows behind us. I can hear her joyful squeals, and a notch of tension unwinds inside my stomach. We're doing what is necessary, but there's no harm in having a little fun too.

The light around Lucas seems to constantly bend and shift, moving around his arms, lighting his path as needed. I wonder if he does this on purpose or if it is an unconscious reaction the light has to his magic.

I hold my tongue. I do not know these people yet. But I hope I get to.

The sound of rushing water reaches us first; then when the trees break, I see the gurgling stream between them. The light skips over it like twinkling stars.

Lucas turns to me when we reach the edge with his mouth open to speak, then tilts his head, puzzled.

"Emmeline," he says quietly. "Where did your shadow go?"

A flash of heat travels from my head to my toes. Most people don't notice when Dar frolics, but of course Lucas would. He is too attuned to the light not to notice a change in its opposite.

Dar! I scream in my head, not sure if she can hear me. I forgot that she was playing behind us, only tethered to me by a thin thread.

"What do you mean?" I say, twirling my skirt, and praying Dar gets the message.

Sorry, she murmurs as she slides up behind me, doing her best to appear to have been hidden by my skirts.

Lucas stares, then scratches his head. "I—I must be seeing things," he says. "Anyway, here's how you collect the water."

I knew we had a well on our estate, but until now I never stopped to consider that our servants had to retrieve countless buckets of water every day. Lucas demonstrates how to fill each bucket and not spill a drop. I mimic his motions, but I am not as coordinated.

Lucas watches me, and when I spill the second bucket of water on my feet, drenching my skirts in the process, he bursts out laughing. I'm almost surprised; he finds so much merriment in everything, even the most menial tasks. He is very different from the handful of other children I met at our estate, and certainly nothing at all like Kendra. Even Dar only finds real amusement in our shadow games.

"You have to move in smoother motions. Try it again, but go slower. Don't overthink it."

I sigh but lean over once again to fill one of the buckets. Lucas puts a steadying hand on my elbow as I twist to fill the second bucket too. This time I manage to fill them both, only sloshing a small amount over my toes. Working together, it seems, is the answer.

"Well done! Now the hard part—not spilling it all on the trek home."

Lucas grins, and I groan. "I fear this may not go well."

"Just follow my feet; step where I step, and it will be fine."

The wind toys with my hair, tossing it in my face while I struggle to keep the buckets level. But Lucas is right; he does know the best route. Following his footsteps helps and gives me something to focus on.

Dar sidles up to me and curls around one of the buckets. Dark lines wrinkle through her form, and I think that means she's frowning.

These tasks are boring. When can we play again?

I pause, letting Lucas get a little farther ahead of me before daring to respond. "You'll have to play without me while we're here. We can't tell them about you yet. Not until we're both sure we can trust them," I whisper.

Dar sighs and slides off the bucket. She bores so easily. I wish she could find joy in simple things like this, the way Lucas seems to.

"Are you all right?" Lucas calls back at me.

"Yes, sorry. Pebble in my shoe."

Lucas waits for me halfway up the hill, the sun dancing through his hair, while I retrace his steps. I'm sure I missed some of them. I'll have to be more careful.

Being out in the world is harder than I thought.

I have not yet told Lucas I'm a shadow weaver, but if I'm going to stay with his family and not lose my mind, I must eventually. My mother's words ring in my ears: *don't be an embarrassment.* My talent set them up for ridicule and censure. And it cost me the lone human friend I thought I had in Kendra.

The only one who doesn't fear my magic is Dar.

By the time we get to the top of the hill, I'm exhausted and my feet ache. But Lucas seems to have boundless energy as though he lives on sunlight alone.

He leads me to the water basin they keep near the shed, and we empty our buckets. I happily hand mine over to him, and he puts them away while I collapse in the shade and stretch out my arms on the grass. My fingers twitch, wanting nothing more than to knead the shadows at the edge of the woods into something fun. A bird, or maybe this time a cat.

Before I realize what I've done, the shadows are inching toward me.

"Emmeline, my mum wants us to weed the garden now," Lucas calls. I snap back to reality, shoving the shadows away to where they belong. I sit up quickly, heart thundering in my ears as I examine his face. He shows no sign that he saw me doing anything strange. Dar grumbles in my ears.

I get to my feet, wiping leaves from my dress, and follow Lucas to the other side of the cottage where the garden sits. Row upon row of brown earth and reaching green fronds line the space. Some areas are boxed out by pieces of wood, and others—like the tomato plants—are raised up on trellises, already heavy with fruit.

Every single leaf gives off a shadow in the late morning sun, striking a pang in my chest.

"You never tended a garden before?" Lucas asks.

I shake my head. I haven't the slightest idea where to start. Yet another thing I took for granted on the estate.

He wrinkles his brow. "What kind of servant were you, anyway?"

Be careful, Dar warns as her dark form slinks over my toes.

I square my shoulders, hoping I don't let my uneasiness show. "I was a ladies' maid. We didn't get our hands dirty much, except occasionally with laundry."

"Nothing very useful then?"

"Only if you need your hair done up," I say, feeling oddly proud of myself and disgusted at the same time. How can I expect them to know me and accept me when I can't even be honest with them regarding the most basic things about myself? But there's just too much at stake right now.

Lucas laughs. "Ask my mum about that." I freeze, sincerely hoping he does not mention it to his mother. The truth is, I know nothing about putting up hair. I haven't even had a servant do mine in years. A simple brushing has worked fine for me.

He kneels down in the dirt beside a row. Judging by the long greens hanging from them, I'm guessing this row is green beans. "So, Mum wants us to do some weeding. They're finicky things and keep sprouting up every week. It's important to stay on top of it so the real plants have room to grow. Pa sells the vegetables at the market, and Mum makes things from her herbs, like the poultice she used on you, to sell too."

I kneel down next to him.

"See this plant here?" He points to the one I believe to be green beans.

"Yes."

"That's a vegetable. We want to keep that. But this one"— he points to a smaller plant consisting of two long green leaves shooting up from the earth—"is a weed. So, pull these, not the first ones."

"I can manage that."

"Good, because Mum wants us to weed this whole thing today." He sweeps his arm out, indicating the entire garden plot.

"That's a lot."

He nods sagely. "It's not the most fun, but it's only once a week. Tomorrow I get to practice baking again."

"I'm happy to help," I say, meaning it wholeheartedly. They've given me food, clothing, and shelter, not to mention protection from the soldiers. Pulling up some weeds is the least I can do.

We get to work, side by side at first, then spreading out in opposite directions. I sneak occasional glances at Lucas, marveling at his behavior. He treats me like we're equals, just two children on any normal day.

It is a jolting thing to realize that no one has ever treated me that way before.

The sun beats down, and soon my hair sticks to my face and my hands are coated in dirt. But there is something about doing this work, something about making the rows more orderly and neat that appeals to me. I can see progress has been made, and by the time I'm halfway across the yard, I stand up to survey my work.

The greens and the shadows dance together in the breeze, almost as if they say thank you.

Suddenly something cool and sticky hits my face. Startled, I brush it away only to find my hand covered with more dirt— and to see Lucas on the other side of the garden grinning.

"It's just some weeds."

Laughter bubbles up in my throat, and I grab a fistful from my own pile of weeds and lob it toward him. It doesn't make it nearly far enough, so I grab another and run after him. He ducks and weaves throughout the garden, knowing the way better than me, but finally I score a hit.

With weeds in his hair, he folds his arms. Then deftly pulls some he had hidden in his pockets and tosses them at me.

"Oh!" I cry, batting them away. We run around the garden, lobbing bits of earth and discarded weeds back and forth until we're exhausted and our stomachs hurt from laughing. Lucas collapses underneath one of the trees at the edge of the yard and leans against the trunk. I settle next to a nearby tree too. Its shadow bends toward me, but I resist reaching out.

Dar slides over to it in greeting, but I can't tell her to stop with Lucas so close.

Emmeline, we ought to run off and play in the woods. I can hide you so that they never find you... Dar stops just shy of the tree's shadow, directing her attention to me, but I cannot return it just yet.

"Truce," Lucas says holding his empty hands out. I giggle.

"Truce," I agree.

He sighs at the mess we've made of the garden. "We're going to have to clean that up, you know."

"We should probably get started then," I say. I busy my hands by winding a blade of grass around one finger, but it isn't the same as the feel of shadows.

Lucas sits bolt upright. "We should. But first, I want to show you something."

I raise an eyebrow. "Show me what?"

He gets to his feet and offers me a hand. I take it, and he pulls me up, Dar grumbling behind me. When he lets go, my skin is still warm from the gentle pressure of his fingers on my wrist.

We walk back to the garden, but at a slower pace this

time. Lucas stands over one of the first patches we cleared in the garden—the green beans—and begins to sing.

The music wraps around the garden and the light around us bends and plays in response. The temperature rises a few degrees, and I roll up my sleeves.

Oh, I don't like this at all, Dar says so quietly that I barely hear her. But I'm too distracted by the sight before me to give it much thought.

Lucas brings the light down, closer to the ground, but keeps it hazy instead of focused like when he was toasting the croissants. I gasp in amazement as the green beans begin to swell and grow, new leaves opening up and the vegetables sprouting before my eyes.

"Incredible," I breathe. For a brief moment, I am a little jealous. His talent is much more useful than mine. So many applications, so much good he can do with it.

I am certain no one has ever told him he and his magic are anything less than a wonder.

In mere minutes the beans are long and fat and ready to be harvested. Together we pick them until our basket is full, then we bring them inside to give to his mother. When she sees them, she laughs.

"Showing off, are we, Lucas?"

His cheeks redden, and he scuffs his toe. She ruffles his hair and takes the basket from him, setting it on the counter.

"Care to explain why you two are all dirty?" she asks.

Now both of our cheeks flame, and suddenly the floor is intensely fascinating.

Miranda sighs and peeks out the back door, then gasps. "Really? You made such a mess. Go clean that up right—"

But she doesn't get to finish what she was saying. Her stern words are cut off by a sharp rapping at the front door of the cottage.

CHAPTER TEN

Miranda freezes, one hand still pointing at the garden. Then she moves like lightning, closing and locking the back door, yanking the curtains closed, and ushering the two of us toward their bedroom. She tosses a rug aside and unlatches a trapdoor, revealing a crawl space inside.

"Lucas, you know the drill. Stay in there until I come get you and don't say a word. Don't make a sound, and definitely do not use any magic, not even a tiny bit."

The rapping at the door continues, growing more insistent with every second. Lucas has paled. His father appears in the doorway, then vanishes as his mother nods.

Lucas climbs down and I follow after him. His mother closes the trapdoor gently and replaces the rug. She even drags a chair over it for good measure.

Every breath feels like I'm swallowing knives.

Why is Miranda scared of someone at their door? Lucas did mention earlier on the way to the river that his parents had instructed him never to talk to strangers. But they are taking it far more seriously than I would have expected. Though I am grateful for it; I have people I wish to hide from too.

My stomach churns as we huddle down in the crawlspace. Dar slinks through the cracks, and I feel her gliding across my shoulders, offering me comfort. I wrap her around me, thankful it is too dark for Lucas to see her.

We don't say a word. When we hear the front door open and Lucas's father says hello, we stop breathing. As if a single wayward breath could give us away to this faceless enemy.

A man's voice rumbles from the doorway. "We are looking for a girl," he says. My heart flies into my throat, throbbing like it wishes to run free. "She is about this high with dark hair and eyes. She's..." The man hesitates. "A little bit strange."

I ball my hands into fists and bite down on a knuckle. Lucas puts a hand on my arm and squeezes.

It's the soldiers, I'm sure of it. That voice sounds like Tate's nephew, Alden. I'm at the mercy of Lucas and his family now.

If they betray us, Dar says, *I'll find a way to protect you. I promise.*

I lean into her comforting presence, and put my hand over Lucas's.

"Why? Is she lost?" Alfred says.

Alden jumps on this excuse. "Yes, sir. And her parents miss her keenly. They're offering a reward to anyone who has information that brings her home."

I'm not ready to go back. I miss home, but it won't be the same until I have set right what went wrong. Dar will fix everything once the ritual to make her whole again is completed.

If the soldiers come for me, I will flee before they can take me.

Miranda chimes in. "A girl? Alfred, didn't we see a child in the woods yesterday matching that description? She was all alone, too."

"We did indeed. She was across the river, but it appeared she was headed toward Zinnia, if I'm not mistaken."

"Zinnia?" Alden says, surprise coloring his voice.

"I believe so. She was definitely traveling away from us. Perhaps she stopped at the local village about a mile away. Have you tried there?"

"We just came from the village this morning. Regrettably, no one has seen her."

"Well, head for Zinnia and you're bound to find her."

"We'll do that," Alden says. "Thank you."

"Good luck," Miranda says. "I hope you find her. It must be awful to lose a child like that."

When the door closes, my heart stutters back to its normal pace. But a sick feeling still fills me. I will have to explain to Lucas and his family why Alden and his men are after me.

They lied for me. They protected me. Not even my own parents could do that. The least I can do is tell them the truth.

It feels like an eternity passes before we finally hear the rug being moved aside and the latch on the trapdoor opening. Light assails us, making me wince, but Lucas appears to be given new life by it. I forgot; darkness may suit me, but for someone with light magic it must be uncomfortable to sit in the shadows for long.

Alfred pulls him up and envelops him in a bear hug, while Miranda holds out a hand to help me up. I can't meet her eyes. She must know I haven't told them everything, that I'm keeping something back.

"Lucas," she says, "go set the table for lunch please."

"But Mum…"

"Go. Now."

He casts a nervous glance in my direction then heads to the kitchen. His parents study me. My stomach drops into my boots.

This is it. They're going to send me home. They're going to tell me to leave, at the very least.

They are quiet for a moment, exchanging a look. Miranda speaks first.

"Emmeline, those men were here seeking a girl whose description sounded a lot like you."

I stare at my feet. Dar whispers in my ear, *Please don't tell. Keep me secret for now.*

Of all the people I've met, I suspect Lucas's family is

among the few who might believe me about Dar, but I won't betray my best friend.

"We have secrets of our own, as you may have guessed when we hid you and Lucas," Alfred adds. "We're not going to force you to tell us anything you don't want to."

"We want to trust you, and we want you to trust us," Miranda says. "We've already placed a lot of faith in you by letting you stay here, and Lucas has too. He revealed his talent to you, however unintentionally."

Unspoken words tie my tongue in knots. I twist my hands together, wishing like never before that I could throw up a wall of my shadows and hide. Being caught by Lord Tate was awful, but this feels a hundred times worse.

Miranda places a hand on my shoulder and squeezes. "You seem like a sweet girl. Whatever happened to cause you to run away must have been awful. You can stay here for as long as you need to. Maybe we can help you track down a relative who will take you in. But we do hope that you'll confide in us when you're ready. We'll be better equipped to help you if we know what's really going on."

The lump in my throat makes it impossible to swallow. Tears sting my eyes, and their forms swim in front of me.

"Thank you for your kindness," I finally manage to squeak out.

Miranda puts her arms around me and hugs me to her, rendering me fully speechless. No one has hugged me in years—not since the incident with Rose—except for Dar, but this is much more solid and welcoming.

Her arm remains around my shoulders as we leave the room. "Come on, Lucas has been listening at the door anyway, we might as well go have lunch."

I feel warmer and more grateful than I ever have in my life. I think, finally, I have learned what real friends do for each other.

CHAPTER ELEVEN

When night descends and the rest of the household has fallen asleep, Dar curls around my cot, whispering in my ear.

It is time, she says. My stomach tightens.

"For what?"

To begin collecting items for the ritual. There are several things you will need to gather; then on the next full moon you can perform the ritual.

"That's only about a week away."

Indeed, it is.

"What must I do?" I begin to dress. I made a promise, and I intend to keep it. I can't wait to see Dar as a real girl.

Once the ingredients are collected, you will need to combine them into a mixture. Then you must put the concoction on me. As a shadow weaver, you're the only one who can touch my form and make the ritual work.

A hard knot begins to form in my stomach. She needs me far more than I ever realized, but she is here because she's my friend. She has more than proven that over the years.

I lace up my boots and gather my cloak. The darkness is plentiful here in the cottage, and I pull the shadows to me in case any of the family is still awake. Spending an entire day not touching the shadows has been torture.

"What must I collect tonight?" I whisper.

Witch hazel is first.

My heart sinks. "I'll have to go into the woods for that, won't I?"

We'll go together.

I don't relish the idea of venturing into the forest when the guards might return at any time, but the darkness lends me safety.

I won't steer you wrong, Emmeline. I promise. Dar places a shadowy hand on my shoulder. I rest mine over it.

"All right."

We sneak out of the cottage undetected, and Dar directs me to the east to find the witch hazel.

It grows at the edges of fields like the one where you found Lucas, she says.

"Why didn't you say something then?" I frown, peering into the darkness to the east.

Dar grumbles. *That boy and his light. They stole my voice. I don't like it. I don't trust him.*

I bristle. "Lucas's light is beautiful. Don't you see how much I need to know someone else who has magic?" Lucas may prefer the light as much as Dar and I prefer the darkness, but I've never heard him complain about shadows.

She sulks as I walk between the trees, but I grow bolder every minute. The newfound freedom is invigorating. No Mother and Father to tell me no, to insist I come inside and wash up for dinner. Or go to bed. The shadows bend and sway as we pass. Above us, the stars wink through the branches. I pretend I'm dancing with them all the way to the field where I found Lucas.

Dar is silent.

I pause between the trees at the edge of the field. My breath catches at the sight. The long grass buzzes with life, and the moon paints all the flowers in glowing silver.

The night and darkness still own my heart.

"Isn't it beautiful, Dar?"

She wallows at my feet and does not answer.

"Don't be angry, please? Why can't I have both you and Lucas?" I fold my arms over my chest. "Besides, once the ritual is done, we'll go home and set things right. This is only temporary."

The truth of my words makes my chest ache in a way I hadn't expected. I will not know him for long. Once I'm home again, everything will go back to normal—and for me, normal means I will pass my days in my room, alone with my shadows and Dar.

But that's what I wanted, isn't it?

Dar sighs. *I worry you will get attached to him and...and that you'll leave me behind once I'm flesh again.*

"Oh, Dar, I'd never do that. You're my best friend. You know that." I smooth over the edges of her wispy form and she billows with relief.

Promise?

"Yes, I promise I'll never leave you."

She curls around my neck and settles in. *Then let's find that witch hazel.*

"What does it look like?" I ask.

It's an odd bush, with yellow and orange flowering fronds. You'll know it when you see it.

I trust her to guide me, and we set out around the edge of the field. Somewhere in the distance a wolf howls, but it doesn't faze me in the slightest. My shadows will protect me, I'm sure of it.

Halfway around the field, I spy an odd-looking plant, just as Dar described. "Is that it?" I point to it.

Yes! Dar says, her excitement fizzing through my skin.

I break into a run, the shadows I've collected on my trek trailing behind me like ribbons. The patch of shrubs is almost as tall as me, and the blossoms are just as strange as Dar said. The shadow it casts on the forest floor looks like a shaggy beast. I can't help but reach out and pet the shadow. It shivers in the night breeze at my touch, but I let it rest where it is.

"How much should I take?"

A few blossoms, to be safe.

I pluck four of them from the bush and twirl them between my fingers. "Such odd things. And yet, they will help us fix everything."

I feel Dar's grin on the back of my neck. *I cannot wait.*

"Neither can I." I tuck the flowers into my skirt pocket. "What else can we gather tonight?" My success at this task has cleared all the sleep from my head. I'm ready to do whatever needs doing right now.

Nothing else tonight. We must gather the items in just the right order and one at a time.

I pout. "Oh, then it might take some time to complete?"

Not long. We're off to a good start. We have more days until the blood moon than items we need, so if all goes well, we might even be ready early. Dar wriggles at my feet, and I know she's pleased.

"Then we'd best get back to the cottage before we're missed."

I run straight across the field this time, reveling in the feel of the wind on my cheeks and the smooth blades of long grass under my outstretched palms. Dar laughs as she whips behind me. We slow when we reach the trees, moving more carefully in case we stumble upon anyone camped out in the woods.

We can never be too safe, not until we've made things right. And tonight we are one step closer to doing just that.

When the cottage comes into sight, I pull my shadows back around me and creep low to the ground. The last thing I need is for Lucas or his parents to glance out a window and see me running through their yard, especially after the incident with the soldiers this afternoon. But the garden and trees dotting the yard give me cover and soon I am at the front door. Ever so carefully, I turn the knob and push it open. It creaks slightly, and I hold my breath. No one stirs.

Don't you want to know what they're hiding? Dar says as we pass by Alfred's study, the door closed as always. *They must be hiding something terrible about Lucas if they make him hide at the first hint of a stranger.*

"To be fair, we're hiding things too," I whisper. "And there is nothing terrible about Lucas."

Still we ought to know who it is we're staying with. We need to know why they take such care to keep Lucas hidden from those guards. If they're in some kind of trouble, that puts us in danger too.

I frown. "I doubt they're in trouble. They're just protective."

But Dar's suggestion niggles at me, eating away at my resolve.

My curiosity wins out. These are good people, and they must have a reason to be wary. I'll just have to prove it to Dar, that's all.

No one is awake, and it is ever so tempting… I'll just see if the door to the study is locked.

A quick check finds the knob twisting under my hand unexpectedly. I slip inside the room, closing the door softly behind me. The room is just as I'd expect—a desk sits in the center, and the walls are lined with books. Alfred always seems to have one in his hands. A window looks out onto the woods and the shadows waving through the trees.

"See? Nothing out of the ordinary, Dar."

As far as you can see. What's on the desk?

A sheaf of papers is strewn over the oak furniture, and I get a closer look. They appear to be receipts for items they bought at the market.

Dar has no response but I can sense her disappointment. It's almost as though she wishes they were hiding something after all. I move to leave when something catches my eye. Beneath the desk is a slim drawer. I almost missed it at first. An odd chill runs down my spine, but I shrug it off. It probably contains nothing of importance.

But it wouldn't hurt to check.

I try to pull the drawer open and at first it sticks, though there is no keyhole I can see to make me think it's locked. I tug and tug until I am afraid I'll go flying if it moves.

Check underneath. Dar suggests. *Sometimes there's a hidden latch.*

I do as she says, and sure enough on the underside of the desk there's a small lever that's easy to miss. I pull the lever and the drawer releases. My stomach flutters, and I examine the contents of the drawer, feeling more than a little guilty.

It seems to be more of the same—at least until my hand lights on a small, old scroll tucked far into the back of the drawer. I pull it out and spread it on the table.

A thrill ripples through Dar.

The scroll is a very long list of names, written in many different hands—some very old and others definitely new—followed by locations and what must be dates. Some of the names, especially the older ones, are crossed out. I pore through the whole thing, and that is it. Just many, many names.

Well that is certainly intriguing. Who do you think these people are on the list?

"I haven't the slightest idea," I say, the hair raising on the back of my neck. "But I think we need to put it back right away."

I shove the scroll back into the drawer, unable to escape the feeling that eyes are tracking my every movement.

"They have a list of people. So what? It doesn't mean anything. It could simply be a list of their family members." The idea settles into place in my mind. "Yes, I think that must be it. And someone must have been tracking the family for some time. Why else would the names be in many different hands and there be so many different places?"

Dar hums. *It could be, I suppose.*

"It is," I say. "It's the only explanation that makes sense."

If you say so.

I push away the creeping doubt. Lucas and his family know what it is like to have a talent. Every word and deed from them says clearly that I can trust them. I can't let something silly like this make me doubt them.

I close up the study, careful to leave it just as I found it. Then I tiptoe back through the hall to my cot, and curl up with the witch hazel safely tucked away in my flour sack.

"What do we tell them if they find the witch hazel?" I whisper to Dar.

They won't.

"But what if they do?"

Tell them nothing. It's an unusual flower you picked when you came across it.

I digest Dar's suggestion in silence. I do not like the idea of lying to Lucas and his family when they've been so kind to me, but I know what happens when people hear that I talk to my shadow. Attempting to make my shadow flesh would surely be even worse.

The hard lump in my gut tightens. However much I loathe lies, I admire Lucas and his family far too much to tell them the whole truth. But maybe I can share something. Lucas trusted me enough to show me how he works with light. And his parents lied to protect me from those guards. That list is just a list, nothing more.

Maybe tomorrow I will tell them about my shadowcraft.

CHAPTER TWELVE

The next morning, I am exhausted again yet filled with purpose. I have made up my mind to tell Lucas and his family what I am, what I can do. But I won't tell them about Dar. Not until she agrees.

She is not happy with my decision and has been sulking at my feet all morning. I suppose, in some way, it's good she's acting like a normal shadow for once.

After the soldiers came to the cottage yesterday, Alfred tracked them to ensure they are not hanging around. He found no trace of them, save a day-old campfire. When he returned, he and Miranda retreated into the study with grim faces.

I can appreciate why they don't advertise Lucas's talent,

but I'm terribly curious to know why his family fears these soldiers. I hope they'll confide in me too. Maybe that list I found last night does have something to do with it, but I don't believe its existence is as sinister as Dar does.

There are just as many good reasons to hide something as there are bad reasons.

Lucas and I weren't allowed outside at all yesterday afternoon because the soldiers might be close, but today he sneaks me out to the same field in which I first saw him, and where I gathered the witch hazel last night. It is his favorite place to practice his light singing—there's no one around for miles, and he can use the light in any way he wants without worry of being seen or accidentally setting their cottage on fire.

Dar grumbles the whole way even though it isn't far.

Why must he screech and use that blinding stuff? What a terrible, unpleasant talent. I sigh and try to ignore her. It is much easier to listen to Lucas's happy banter.

He sits in the middle of the field, the long grasses bowing toward him like they know him and the light he brings. I meander around the field, letting Dar skitter through the little shadows cast by the grasses and flowers, and run my hands over the lacelike blossoms of white and gold. They feel like velvet under my fingertips.

When Lucas begins to sing, it is as though the sun has come out from behind a cloud we didn't know was there. He crafts the light into an orb with his song, making it expand and contract with a nudge of his pitch. It is brilliant and warm. But I can't settle down and bask in it. The restless need to keep moving consumes me and I circle the field, getting ever closer to Lucas and where he sits in the center.

Dar has gone silent, falling deeper into her sulk as the shadows grow thinner and thinner in the field. The pull toward the light is magnetic, and soon I am close enough to feel the heat of it. It pulses now, responding to the notes in the song, and reminds me of a bubble close to bursting.

The light is so beautiful that I want to reach out and touch it. It's almost as lovely as my shadows.

Lucas has shared his secret with me, and I want to share mine with him. Dar has nothing to say on this. With all the light, she barely shrouds the edges of my feet. I know she doesn't like this feeling, but I can't resist the kindness of Lucas and his family. It is more than my own has ever shown me, and I don't think they'll fear me either.

I hope.

Lucas finishes his song and glances shyly in my direction.

I grin, the sun warming my limbs and filling me up with a strange tingling sensation. "That was incredible," I say.

He stares at his feet, red blotches dotting his cheeks.

My breath stutters, but I force the words I need to say from my mouth. "There is something I'd like to show you."

Lucas tilts his head toward me in curiosity, letting me take the center of the field. I hold out my hands, calling out the shadows in the forest surrounding us. First they quiver. Then they soar through the air like ribbons of smoke. I pull them around me, enjoying the feel of my shadows after so many hours without them.

I mold and shape them into two forms, starting with dusky shapes that elongate, then sprout four legs and paws. Smoky ears that stand at attention, a tail that quirks with curiosity, and a long snout that could sniff out rabbits. I set the twin forms on the ground and they sniff each other with their shadow snouts, then begin to tussle and romp through field.

I rest my arms at my sides, feeling a little drained. I'm pleased with my work, but my stomach twists into knots. My palms turn slick, and I wipe them on my skirt while I study Lucas's face. He gapes at me and the playing shadow dogs.

Then, finally, he breaks into a wide grin.

"You have shadow magic." He takes a step closer, reaching a hand out as the dogs tumble past him. "Just like I have light magic. What do you call it?"

"Shadow weaving," I say, feeling oddly bashful all of a sudden.

"It's wonderful!" He laughs at the shadow dogs as they roll in the grass at our feet.

I blink a few times to quell the burning sensation forming behind my eyes. I've been told countless times to hide my talent, to use it sparingly, not to talk about it—I can't recall anyone ever telling me my magic is wonderful, except for Dar.

A spark of something warm and happy blooms under my ribs. I was right to trust Lucas.

But has he really told you everything? Dar whispers. *These people are hiding something, I am certain of it.*

I brush off Dar's concerns. She hates Lucas's light, but he

doesn't hate my shadows. He sees the wonder in my talent, just like I see the wonder in his. Lucas's immediate acceptance has only made Dar's snide comments about his magic feel all the more petty.

"I'm glad you think so," I say to Lucas. "Not everyone feels the same."

"But your craft is exceptional. I've been working with my light singing for years, and I can't yet make anything quite as detailed as you can."

"I've had a lot of time to practice. Where I come from, people fear me and my magic. Even my parents." I glare at the flowers in the field.

"Your parents? They sent you into servitude because of it?" he frowns.

Careful, Emmeline, Dar warns.

Drat, I'd nearly forgotten my original lie. I do not like this whole lying business; it is too hard to keep track of the things you've made up.

"Not exactly. I wasn't quite honest with you that first day, Lucas, and I apologize for that. I wasn't sure I could trust you. I didn't want you to be scared of me." I nudge a clump of dirt kicked up by the playing dogs. "Or worse, make me go back home."

Lucas goes very still, and something prickles over my skin, like I can feel the whisper of fear that runs through him.

"I am not a servant, you see. I don't work on the estate over the hills; my parents own it. They were going to send me away because they hate my magic." I swallow hard. Just the thought of being cured like Simone and losing my shadows is chilling.

Lucas puts a hand on my shoulder. "That's horrible. How could your parents hate something so wonderful?"

I shrug helplessly. "My parents were embarrassed by what I could do and a little scared too. They didn't even give me a choice. They insisted I had to leave because I was ruining their lives. Instead I fled. I will choose where I go, not them."

I'm not yet ready to tell him about Dar, or admit what happened with Lord Tate, especially how it was my fault. Perhaps I'll tell him everything later. One small step at a time is best; I can tell Dar is furious I've told him as much as I have already.

"We won't make you go back. I promise. My parents... well they'd have some choice words for yours, I'm sure."

"We don't need to tell them what I can do. Do we?"

He nods firmly. "We do." Then he grins. "They'll think it's wonderful too, and we'll keep you safe."

Relief trills over me like the whisper of butterfly wings.

"Come on," he says, grabbing my hand with warm fingers, sending a pleasant shiver up my arm. "Let's tell them now. Then we'll have to clean up the mess we made in the garden yesterday."

I groan. I'd almost forgotten about our weed and dirt fight after the scare with the soldiers. But Lucas tugs me along, and we run together through the woods, my shadow dogs racing us all the way back the cottage. His eyes brighten when he realizes they've come with us.

Lucas gestures to them when we slow to a stop in the cottage yard. "I suppose that is one way to tell my parents."

My cheeks redden. "I hadn't thought of that. Do you think we should—"

But it is already too late. Miranda is in the garden, humming and pulling up potatoes for dinner when she sees us. She straightens up just as one of the shadow dogs barrels towards her.

Startled, she drops her potato and scrambles backward.

Lucas begins to laugh, but my stomach tightens, and I chase after them.

Tsk, tsk, tsk, Dar says.

My heart sinks. It was foolish of me to keep the shadow dogs outside of the field. I wave a hand and the one pawing at Miranda's foot dissipates into smoke.

"I'm so sorry!" I cry, rushing up to her. Lucas manages to hold in his laughter and appears at my side.

"What was that?" she asks, dusting off her apron.

Lucas nudges me with his shoulder. I can barely look up from my feet.

"Emmeline has something to tell you," he says.

His mother's voice softens. "What is it, Emmeline?"

Blood thrums in my ears. How many times has it been pummeled into my head not to tell or show strangers my magic? Too often to count.

Lucas nudges me again.

"I haven't been wholly honest with you," I say. A sick feeling rises in my gut, but I press it down.

"About what exactly?" she asks.

"I have a talent too. Shadow weaving."

"She made those dogs!" Lucas says, but quiets at a single stern glance from his mother.

"Yes, I did. And I'm not a servant either. Those soldiers were looking for a girl who ran away from her parents' estate. That girl is me."

Miranda goes rigid. "Emmeline, why did you run away from your home?"

Because my shadow did something terrible to the man who wanted to cure me of my magic is what I should say, but instead I tell a half-truth.

"My parents hated my shadowcraft. Even the servants were afraid of me." My hands twist of their own accord. "They were going to send me away. From everything I know and love. Because they were done putting up with me and my talent."

"Oh, sweetheart," Miranda says. She curls an arm over my shoulders and leads me toward the house, her son following close behind. "That's horrible. How can a parent think what makes their child special is something evil, or worse, inconvenient? Those dogs were so lifelike, you nearly scared me to death. If you can craft something that detailed, your talent must be impressive indeed."

She opens the door to the cottage. "Come, show us what you can do, safely away from prying eyes."

I hesitate in the doorway. "You won't make me go home?"

She sighs. "No. Not yet anyway. And only if you decide that's what you want to do."

A small sob escapes from my lips before I can hold it back. "Thank you," I say.

Perhaps they are not so bad after all, Dar whispers.

CHAPTER THIRTEEN

After breakfast the next morning, we set out for the nearby village. Alfred and Miranda debated about whether to bring me along at first since the guards might still be on the lookout, but in the end they decided it was better to keep me close than leave me home alone. Plus, Miranda is determined to get me a dress that actually fits. The family runs a market stall in the village with fresh vegetables, thanks to Lucas's talent.

The villagers don't know of this, of course, and I've been strictly instructed not to mention Lucas's light singing or to reveal my shadow weaving while we're there. Just to be safe, they said.

I could not agree more, Dar whispers in my ear. *Our best defense right now is to not attract attention.*

Once we reach the path, it is easy going, but at first we have to wind our way through grasping bushes and around tall, thick trees. Lucas and I run ahead, and every once in a while, he lets loose a burst of his light magic, much to the annoyance of his parents.

"Lucas!" his mother hisses. "Stop showing off. We'll arrive at the village soon."

Up ahead, the path turns, and when I reach the curve in the road, I see it. The village is surrounded by an apple orchard. Houses dot the outer edges, becoming larger and closer together as they near the village center. The houses on the outskirts have thatched roofs, but bright red and green tiles shine on the tops of the taller buildings farther in.

Alfred and Miranda take us straight to the center of the town where the market is held. Waving banners of all colors adorn the stalls, and the many smells of food and spices and flowers blend together in a strangely beautiful cacophony.

Imagine the games we could play in this crowd, Dar says with a hint of longing in her voice.

"Mum says you have to go with her to the seamstress for some clothes, but let me show you Pa's stall first," Lucas says, grabbing my hand.

He leads me over to where his father is setting up his stall, piling the vegetables he brought in his cart on the counter.

"Lucas, don't go running off today." His father waggles his finger at him. "I need you here to help me."

Miranda puts her hands on my shoulders. "Come, Emmeline, let's get you some new clothes." She frowns. "Are you feeling all right today? You're looking paler than usual this morning."

I shrug. "I feel fine. Just a little tired, I suppose."

Miranda puts a palm on my forehead, but soon straightens up, satisfied. "All right then, let's get going."

Lucas waves as his mother leads me away. We pass by cart after cart of strange goods—antiques and food and jewels, even scrolls and books. Miranda greets a dizzying number of people, shaking hands and inquiring after their families along the way. Finally, she stops just past the market at a black brick building with flounces of fabric in the windows.

My parents never took me to the village near them. They

always had the seamstress come to us, and they made sure she only saw me and took my measurements in their sitting room once I had cleared it of any lingering shadow toys. Fear seizes me for a brief moment. What if this is the village closest to my parents' estate? What if the seamstress recognizes me? I grip the doorway tightly, but when Miranda gives me a look, I relax.

"Are you sure you're all right?" she says.

I paste a happy expression on my face. "Of course."

She seems very suspicious of you this morning, Dar says. *Maybe you shouldn't have told her about your talent after all.*

I swallow my retort to Dar. We'll talk about this later. Instead, I take a deep breath and step inside the store, the door clanking closed behind me, punctuated by the sharp ring of a bell.

My hands have gone slick, and I wipe them on my skirt. A woman I've never seen before pops out from the back room and smiles when she sees us.

"Oh, Miranda, who is this pretty little one?"

Lucas's mother greets her warmly. "My niece. She's come to stay with us for a little while, but I'm afraid her baggage ended up in the river on the journey here. All ruined. She needs a new dress." Even as Miranda speaks, her keen dark eyes take in the store, always on alert. I wonder if it's because she has begun to feel protective of me.

See? Dar whispers. *She lies too easily.*

I try not to bristle at Dar's words. Was she always this suspicious of everyone we met and I just didn't notice? Or has spending this time with Lucas and his family only thrown it into sharp relief?

"Poor thing," the seamstress says, patting me on the head. "That must have been frightful."

I clear my throat and clasp my hands before me. "Yes, it was ma'am."

"So polite too." She takes my arm and leads me toward the back room. I can't help staring at row upon row of bolts of cloth and spools of ribbon lining the walls in a rainbow of colors and shades. At first it seems lovely, then an unsettling feeling runs through me as I remember how Dar told me she died and became a lost soul. It was in a shop just like this. For a moment, I tense, worried this place will trouble her, but she does not say a thing about it, though she is huddled quite close to my feet.

I'm told to stand on a raised platform while the seamstress

pokes, prods, and bends my arms and legs into odd angles to ensure she gets the right measurements. All the while Dar grumbles in my ears about how much she wishes to go outside and play with the shadows instead of mimicking my bizarre motions.

I wish we could make something from the shadows hidden in the nooks and crannies here. There are so many that no one would notice.

A slight shake of my head is all I can give in answer. Hiding is what we must do at all costs. Though I can't help thinking it seems odd that Dar wants to play in a place that ought to conjure up horrific memories for her.

When the seamstress is finally done, it is time to pick the colors. She holds up a pale pink cotton, and I unconsciously wrinkle my nose. Miranda shakes her head immediately.

"No, I don't think so. What do you say, Emmeline?"

"I'm grateful for this; any color will do." I don't quite feel right being choosy when I am at the mercy of their kindness.

"But do you like this one?"

"It is probably not what I would choose for myself."

Miranda laughs. "You are too sweet for your own good. I could see you in this green here"—she plucks the edge of a roll of fabric—"or this blue." She taps another. I run my hands over each of them, smiling. The green is deep, the color of emeralds, and the blue reminds me of the sky at midnight. Nearby is a deep purple, and I pull that down too. It is the color of twilight.

"That settles it, then. Purple."

"Very good," the seamstress says. "It'll be ready in two days."

As we leave, a tightness constricts around my lungs, until it almost hurts to breathe. "I cannot thank you enough," I say to Miranda. "This is terribly generous of you."

"It just wouldn't do to have you wearing ill-fitting dresses while you're here. I'm sure that one isn't comfortable at all. And we're happy to help you." She pulls out a ribbon she bought from the shop. "Hold on for a moment." She pulls my dark hair back, her hands running through it in a way that reminds me of Dar. Then she ties it back with the purple ribbon. "There we are. Perfect."

Miranda, like her son Lucas, is so warm that it seems to be a natural thing for her to do. Perhaps this is why Lucas has lightcraft. The magic of the Cerelia Comet transformed his mother's warmth into a talent for her son.

When we enter the market again, a hush has settled over the crowd and vendors. Like they wait for something ominous to happen. Miranda notices it too, and frowns.

"Stay close, Emmeline," is all she says.

We thread through the throng of people in a hurry to reach the vegetable stall. Miranda pushes me behind the stall just as the hush falls over our section.

Soldiers. I spy their green cloaks first. Fear freezes me in place, until Lucas pulls me behind his father and down into their cart.

"We have to hide in here," he whispers, pulling a blanket over the top of the cart. "Just to be safe."

I don't object, but fear lingers on my skin, turning it cold and hot and cold again.

Strange, that Lucas needs to hide too even though they now know the guards are after you, Dar muses.

I agree it is odd, but this is hardly the time to ask. All I know is that this family fears something or someone terribly.

What could they be hiding? Maybe we should check the study one more time tonight…

I shudder. Invading their privacy like that again is not a thing I wish to do.

I don't know how much time passes. But between the heat and the wait, Lucas and I doze, curled up together in the bottom of the cart. When the blanket is finally pulled back, light assails my eyes, disorienting me, but Lucas has no such trouble.

Miranda stands over the cart with a grim expression on her face. "They're gone. We're going home. Stay where you are. Just in case."

The blanket falls back over us and soon the cart begins to move. The background chatter of the marketplace fades, and soon the clatter and bump of the wheels on the path greet us.

We're on our way back to the cottage and safety. Yesterday, I assumed Miranda and Alfred hid Lucas because they were being overly cautious around strangers. But the soldiers were seeking me. This time it was clear that Lucas's family is desperate to hide him from the soldiers, too. Somehow, the soldiers are a threat to them. Dar's voice echoes in my ear: *What could they be hiding?*

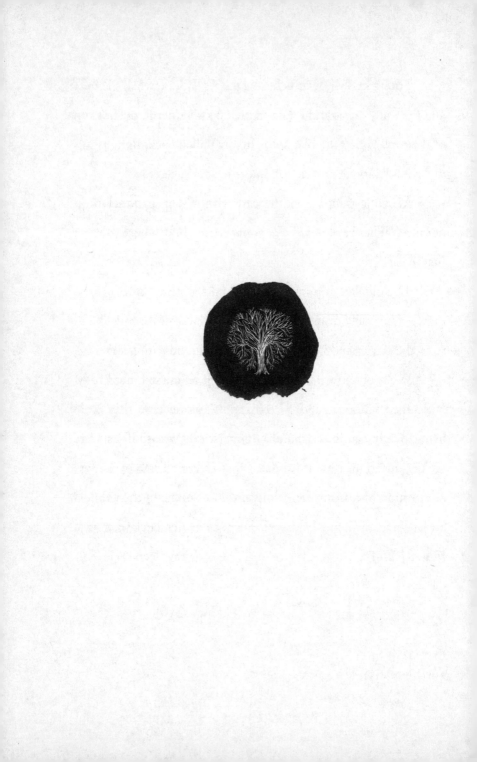

CHAPTER FOURTEEN

That evening when dusk descends, my shadows flock to me as though they have missed me. I have certainly missed them. I don't yet dare play with them as freely as I did at home, even though I've told Lucas and his family about my shadowcraft. But tonight I linger outside even after Lucas has run indoors to set the table. The sky above is clear and bright with stars, and the fireflies beckon to me from between the trees. It energizes me in a way sleep no longer seems to.

Other creatures prowl the woods too. A few keens and howls break the evening calm. I shiver, but Dar wraps around my shoulders.

They won't hurt you. All you have to do is hide in your shadows with me and you'll be safe.

She's right. But I can't yet. Miranda quickly discovered I am useless at helping with dinner, and she has been having me wash dishes instead. It's the least I can do.

My eyes grow hot, and Dar purrs in my ear. *We'll do something nice for them in return once you've performed the ritual. We can thank them together.*

Warmth pours through my limbs. "That sounds like an excellent idea."

Now that we're alone and Dar seems to be in a better mood, I dare to ask the question that has been troubling me all day. "Dar, did the dressmaker's shop upset you at all? I was worried while we were there this afternoon."

A long pause follows, so long that I look down just to be sure Dar did not run off to the woods without me.

It did, she says finally. *But I did not wish you to worry. I could tell you were excited to get the new dress with Miranda, and I didn't want to bother you with it.*

I frown. I'm usually so in tune with Dar's emotions, and she truly seemed to be her normal self at the shop.

And interrupting me with Miranda has never stopped her before.

Could…could Dar be lying to me?

"Dar, what about—"

The cottage door swings open, and Miranda stands there with an odd expression on her face. "Who are you talking to, Emmeline?"

My stomach flips. "No one." I shrug. "I was just playing with a shadow or two."

"Well, you should come in now. It isn't safe to stay outside after dark."

If only she understood that it is the safest place for me. Where the darkness is mine to command. It's where I feel most at home. I stamp down my doubts about Dar and the dress-maker's shop and glide into the cottage, my shadows trailing after me. I leave them at the door with a promise to return later. After all, Dar and I have a ritual to perform and items we must collect.

Later that night, I crawl from my bed and Dar coils around me, hiding my body from view. I lace up my boots and step into the hall. To my surprise, voices echo back to me, hushed whispers coming from the study.

My ears perk and Dar fizzes with curiosity too. I don't need to say a word to know what she wants to do. I confess, so do I. It has been ages since we played my favorite game: eavesdropping. Miranda and Alfred have been warm and welcoming, but Dar has brought up so many suspicions that I can't help feeling disconnected from them still. I wish to know them better.

With my shadows gathered around me, I tiptoe toward the study and find a corner not far from the door to hide in. They won't see me here even if they leave the room, but I can hear them perfectly.

"Don't you see it's gotten worse?" Miranda says and something thumps on the table, but I cannot see what. "Now even Old Winthrop has vanished. I didn't think anyone could get past his talent but someone did. And you know exactly who it was."

Gooseflesh breaks out on my arms, and I pull Dar and my shadows closer. I can hear the steps of someone pacing the room, but I can't tell which of them it is.

Curious, Dar says. *Maybe life isn't as simple here as you believed.*

Part of me bristles at Dar's suggestion that they are up to something sinister, but the rest of me frets.

"Maybe what the villagers are saying is true; maybe he did just retire to another part of the country, one that is sunnier and easier on his old bones."

"Winthrop was important. Alfred, he's a flame breather. Even at his age, he is not one to be trifled with or taken easily."

"All the more reason to believe he wasn't taken at all."

Miranda sighs. "I wish that you were right. But he was the last of those blessed by the comet fifty or more years ago. There's a pattern here. And it scares me. Our plans depended on him."

I back farther into my shadowed corner and wrap my arms around my middle. Dar billows, curiosity getting the better of her.

They are silent for a moment, and while I can't see, I imagine Alfred kisses his wife lightly on the forehead and that she has her arms crossed over her chest. It's a gesture I've seen between them before.

But this time it is not something trivial like running out of carrots for dinner. Someone they know is missing. Someone at the center of some plan they have.

Someone with a fearsome talent. A bead of sweat trickles down my spine, making me shiver.

I told you they're up to something, Dar says, smug satisfaction coloring her tone.

"It doesn't mean it's anything bad," I hiss back. We know only a little about Alfred and Miranda and of course they have lives and plans outside of that. But still, Miranda's mention of many people missing is a thing that sticks to the inside of my brain, never letting go.

If talented people have been going missing, that could be why they hide Lucas from any strangers. But I can't help wondering if this might be connected with Tate and Lady Aisling and their promised cure for talents. I shudder. I would hate to see Lucas's lovely talent disappear almost as much as my own.

Moments later they leave the study, arms interlocked, like they're holding each other up. They head toward their room, and I wait until the door closes softly behind them, then wait a few minutes more for good measure.

We slip out of the cottage into the woods, away from their troubling, mysterious words and ever closer to our goal.

It feels like coming home. The shadows pour forth from the trees at a mere hint of my shadowcraft, like they can sniff me out. Thin shadows of saplings wind around my arms like ribbons, and tiny ones from Miranda's flower garden curl into my hair.

My shadows, my friends, my playmates. These are what my parents wanted to take from me. They are why I had to run away. Something swells in my chest and chokes in my throat.

I cannot bear to give them up.

We have a ways to go tonight, Dar says. *We need to pick an apple.*

"An apple?" I say, almost laughing. Then I remember the orchard outside the local village. "But we can't just take an apple from the orchard. It isn't ours. The villagers sell them in their market."

Unfortunately, this ritual requires the apple to be stolen.

"What sort of ritual would require that?"

Dar sighs and flattens on the ground. *Never mind. I shouldn't have said anything. If you don't want to do the ritual...*

"No! No, of course I do. I want you to be free and whole again." I pull her shape up so she can walk beside me. I can't wait until she can do that on her own two feet.

Are you sure?

"Yes, there is nothing I want more. Let's find that orchard."

The village is to the east, and we head in that direction, guided by the moon and stars.

"How did you find out about this ritual, Dar?" I ask.

I have been waiting for a shadow weaver like you for a very long time, is the only answer she gives.

A twinge of worry presses on my chest, but I do my best to crush it down. I must do this—I want to do this—and I bite my tongue instead of objecting.

The shadows follow us through the trees. It is slow going at first, but soon we reach the path through the woods. It is well hidden, but after Lucas and his family showed it to me, I find it again more easily than I expected.

Though I doubt we'll encounter anyone on the path this late at night, I play it safe and collect all the shadows that have been trailing us, wrapping them around me until I'm fully ensconced in darkness. Out in the forest, night sounds form a chorus of chirps, squeaks, and howls. I tremble, but I'm safe here where no one can see me.

We walk for a long time before signs of civilization begin to appear. A house here, a tilled field there. Lucas and his family certainly do live as far from other people as they possibly can. I wonder if that has anything to do with the plans they mentioned? Though I had resolved not to pry into their secrets, my curiosity is an itch I cannot help but scratch.

My feet begin to ache. I'll have to walk all the way back to the cottage once this task is done, and I'm still tired from the day's adventures.

It isn't far now, Dar says.

I don't reply. I've grown too sour to trust my words to come out in a way that won't be taken badly.

But then the forest thins, and newer, smaller trees come into view. Soon the gnarled forms of the apple trees surrounding the eastern perimeter of the village appear before me, their shadows long and twisted on the ground. Exhausted, I stop to rest for a moment beneath one, tracing the shadow's strange form with my fingertip.

"There are fallen apples all over the place here!" I pick one up. The apples on the ground have begun to rot; the villagers won't miss this one at all.

Dar sighs. *That one isn't good enough. Pick one from the branch, Emmeline. We need it to be fresh.*

I frown. "Let me see if I can find one on the ground that's fresher—"

No, it must be plucked directly from the tree for it to work.

My heart sinks. How can I argue with her, when she knows the ins and outs of the ritual in a way I do not? I only wish stealing wasn't a part of it.

I reach up and grab an apple from the lowest branch, silently promising myself that when this is all done, I will come back and leave some coins under this tree to make up for it.

A branch snaps behind me, and my heart leaps into my throat. Like a fool, I relaxed my grip on the shadows, but now I cocoon them around me and flatten myself against the apple tree.

Stay very still... Dar warns.

I peer into the darkness, and two new forms take shape. A man with his arm outstretched to grip the hand of a woman. They are trying to be quiet too, but the occasional giggle gives them away.

Wait until they have their backs turned. I hold my breath, pulse throbbing in my ears. I can't get caught. If I do, then Lucas's family would send me back home for certain.

I cannot risk that at any cost.

The pair ducks behind one of the thickest-trunked apple trees, and as soon as they do, I make a break for it.

"Who's there?" the man yelps. The sound of my feet hitting the earth is not a thing I can hide with shadow, but even if he turns around, he won't see me. I whisper to one of the sapling's shadows making up my cocoon, "Go."

It wriggles free, and the hole it leaves in my defenses is quickly filled by another shadow spreading farther to cover the space. The loose shadow writhes through the orchard, dodging from tree to tree, giving the couple something else to focus on besides my retreating footsteps. A few yards after I hit the tree line, I release my hold on that shadow, and it flies free back to its rightful place in the forest.

I run, clutching the stolen apple to my chest, despite the pain in my calves and the burning in my lungs. We are halfway to the cottage when my foot snags on a root and I tumble headlong to the ground.

I lay there for a few moments, trying to calm my breath and flying pulse. I shift to a seated position, wincing at my skinned knee. Drat, I shall have to clean that when I get back to the cottage.

And all without waking anyone up.

Tears burn at the corners of my eyes. I can't help wishing there was another way. Something that didn't involve lying and stealing and concealing what I'm really doing. I have no idea what I'll say if Miranda catches me washing up in the wee morning hours.

I only know it can't be the truth.

Dar wraps around my knee, cooling the hot scrape like a cold compress. *I'll help you, you know I will. But we'd best be moving.*

I stumble to my feet and head into the darkness, my guilty conscience following at the heels of my faltering footsteps.

←——•——→

By the time I reach the cottage, I am exhausted. My feet drag, but Dar spurs me onward with whispered words of encouragement.

My knee throbs something awful, pain shooting through my leg with every step.

I cling to the hope that no one is awake. I'm not sure I have the strength to hide myself and be as silent as I usually am.

When I reach the cottage door, I brace myself against it, taking a deep breath. Then I crack it open a hair and listen. Only when I'm satisfied no one is moving about do I step inside.

I must bandage up my knee. Otherwise I'll never be able to sleep. Dar's cool form wrapped around it has helped, but not enough. In the kitchen, I hunt for Miranda's bowls and bandages and poultices that I saw the day I arrived. I find a few of the things I need, then give up on the rest. After I fill a bowl with water from the basin, I settle onto a chair.

Exhaustion crawls over me. I never want to get up. I don't even want to lift my fingers so much as to clean the wound.

Let me help you, Dar says. Her shape writhes and contracts, settling over me in a shape and size identical to mine. When my hand reaches for a cloth, she reaches with me. Because of my magic, she bears a small amount of the burden too.

It isn't much, but at least it's something. And I'm grateful for that.

Wincing at the touch of the wet cloth to my knee, we keep at it until the dirt and grime are gone. As quickly as I can, I bind it up with a bandage. When I'm satisfied with my work, I rinse out the bowl, then dry it carefully and put it back where I found it.

With any luck, Miranda will never know the difference.

Morning wakes me with sleepy bands of light peeking between the curtains of the guest room. I yawn and stretch and swing my legs over the edge of the bed.

My breath hisses between my teeth.

I'd forgotten all about my knee. My discarded clothes are in a pile on the floor where I threw them last night. They're stained with mud. A trail of dirt tracks in from the door.

Heat flashes over my face. If Lucas or his parents see this, they'll know I left the house last night.

We can't risk that, Dar says.

"No, we definitely cannot."

Hurriedly, I shove the dirty clothes under my bed. I'll

have to figure out a way to wash them later. I won't be getting my new dress until tomorrow. I grab a towel from the closet to clean my face in the wash basin then begin scrubbing the floor. Only when the last trace of mud has been removed do I breathe easier again.

I put on a clean but too-large dress, and head for the kitchen. My stomach rumbles. All that walking last night has made me frightfully hungry this morning. The smell of perfectly golden biscuits and scrambled eggs greets me from down the hall, and my feet follow my nose right to it.

The family gathers around the table, but they are oddly silent today. I sit in my chair and reach for a biscuit, only realizing that they all stare at me when it plops on my plate. A cold, hard knot tightens in my gut. Dar hisses in my ear.

"What—what's wrong?" I ask. A wave of dizziness hits me and I'm grateful to be sitting down. My fingernails dig into my knees.

Lucas's parents exchange an unreadable glance. Not angry, but…curious? Annoyed? My pulse spikes.

"Emmeline," Miranda says carefully. "Have you—did you, by any chance, go outside last night?"

I pause midbite.

You mustn't tell them a thing. Pretend you know nothing about it. They must not know about the ritual.

I am sure my face betrays me, but I frown. "No. Why?" I swallow the biscuit, and its buttery flavor curdles in my mouth.

Another hesitant exchange of looks.

They suspect, Dar whispers. *Tell them you sleepwalk. If someone saw you it's the perfect excuse.*

I glance down at my plate, unable to meet their eyes. "At least, not that I know of. I have been known to sleep-walk sometimes."

They relax, and Miranda even lets out a low chuckle. "Well, that would explain it. You do look very tired and pale for so early in the day. It seems you went somewhere quite muddy last night. The kitchen floor was covered in it when I woke up, and dirty footprints led right up to your door."

My mind races, and I gape at the floor. It is pristine now, and I don't recall seeing any footprints in the hall.

She pats my arm. "Don't worry, I cleaned it up already."

"I helped too," Lucas says. "Where do you think you went?"

I do my best to shrug it off, but an undercurrent of fear

pins me to my chair. "Oh, I don't know. If I was muddy, maybe I went to the river."

Alfred's head jerks up, alarm written on his face. "Do you sleepwalk often?"

I shake my head, not wanting to make things worse. "No. I'm sorry. I must have been more restless than I realized last night after the excitement at the market."

"Are you sure? We can take precautions, you know, put a few more locks on the doors. Maybe some bells to make it more likely you'll wake up before you get outside."

The knot in my stomach tightens further. "No please, don't trouble yourselves. I'm sure it was just a one-time thing." The last thing I need is to set off a string of bells while I sneak out in the middle of the night.

Alfred doesn't seem fully satisfied with this answer, but Miranda piles more eggs onto his plate, and he lets it go.

I push my food around with a fork, my appetite waning. I have spent so much time with Dar and her suspicions that it seems incredible Lucas and his parents believe my lie. They are so trusting and open, so different from what I'm used to. They live in the light, while all I've ever known is shadows.

I will have to be more cautious and secretive than ever now so I don't lose that trust.

CHAPTER FIFTEEN

After two recent encounters with the guards, Alfred and Miranda have instructed us to stay close and not venture out to the field where I first glimpsed Lucas. They aren't even letting us fetch water alone. Lucas assures me this is temporary, that they get like this every once in a while, but I can't dispel the lingering sense of guilt that the guards are here for me. Dar's suspicions about their reasons have nearly reached a fever pitch, and I find myself tuning out her remarks more often than not over the course of the morning. It is so much easier to be around Lucas and his light these days than Dar and her dark suggestions.

After Lucas and I finish our chores around the house,

we're allowed to go out into the backyard and play. We have both been dying to practice our talents.

We run out into the open yard, the trees standing guard around us and swaying in the breeze. Lucas doesn't even hesitate; he sings forth his light and begins to shape it. His hands move with the beams as he sings, changing their shape and making them dance across the yard like sparks skittering over the grass. Meanwhile, I pull my shadows close and mold them into a frame over our heads that resembles the gazebos we had on my estate. I take a seat in the shadow swing and kick my legs, the better to watch Lucas's fireworks.

Lucas stops what he is doing and stares at me, slack-jawed.

"How did you do that?" he asks, wonder written on his face. I blush, surprised by his question.

"What do you mean?"

"How did you make your shadows into something tangible like that?"

"You mean you can't do that with your light?" It never occurred to me that this might be unusual. But hidden away as I was in a mansion without so much as chores to keep me busy,

I suppose I have had a lot more time to practice my craft than most talented people.

"No," he says, walking around the smoky gazebo to admire my work. "That's amazing." He pokes at the shadows, and his hand springs back.

Now it is my turn to be surprised.

"You can touch it too?" While I have made many things out of shadow, I don't believe anyone else has ever tried to touch them. I assumed only I could.

Lucas laughs. "I guess I can."

"Maybe it only works like that for talented people like us," I say, marveling.

"Will you show me how to do it with my light?" Lucas asks. "Please?"

Must he know all your secrets? Dar whines. *Next thing you know, you'll be telling him about me, and he'll think you're crazy like everyone else back on the estate.*

A tiny hint of worry wheedles its way into my brain, but I push it down. Helping Lucas work on his magic is not the same as telling him about Dar. I fear she is beginning to get a little jealous of the time I spend with other people, but there's no help for it. I live in their house, and there is little opportunity to be alone except at night. And I enjoy my time with Lucas too—I won't let Dar dampen the happiness of it.

"I can certainly try," I say, grinning back at Lucas.

He moves to stand in front of me with an eager gleam in his eyes. "All right, where do I start?"

How *do* I make the shadows tangible enough to hold my weight? I wave a hand and the shadow gazebo dissolves, but I keep the shadows close at hand to use again.

"Let me see..." I weave the shadows together into something simple. A length of rope. I notice that in the back of my head, I am thinking about it becoming solid. I've done this for so long without realizing it that it has become second nature to me. "First, call your light to you. Then as you mold it, focus on increasing its mass. I tend to think of my shadows as tacky usually, but I've made rope that has held my weight before. It's how I escaped from my parents' estate."

Lucas looks at me with a sort of awe that forces my eyes to the ground. I don't know how to respond to someone regarding me in such a way, especially after babbling on about my shadow weaving.

"Go ahead," I say, not yet looking up. "You try it."

He begins to sing and his light responds. He tries to twist it into bands first, but they remain as ephemeral as before. His hand passes right through them, and his song cuts off.

"Maybe it would help to try something that would normally be solid? Like a rope?"

Lucas's face, discouraged moments before, brightens. "Of course, that makes sense."

"And be sure to keep thinking about how solid it is as you shape it." Hopefully my advice will help and not discourage him further.

He makes another attempt, and another, but he seems to have trouble molding the light into a specific object. I've only seen him turn it into bands or orbs or a diffuse cloud so far.

After the third attempt, Lucas sinks onto the grass, frustrated, and begins to yank up the green blades fistfuls at a time. The light that usually animates him seems to fade. I want to help him bring it back.

"Why don't you try closing your eyes while you do it? And picture the light turning into pieces of twine? Start small. Just a little bit of light at first, then build from there."

Maybe he just isn't as good as you, Emmeline, Dar says with a yawn. I can tell she is getting bored already. I'll have to practice more of my own craft soon so she'll have a chance to play too.

"Is that how you do it?" he asks. "Visualize like that?"

"Yes, I think so. I barely remember when I began to make my shadows have more heft to them, but visualizing should help."

"All right, fine. I'll try one more time," Lucas says. He gets to his feet again, dusting off his trousers and brushing the dirt from his hands.

This time when he sings, he closes his eyes, and his entire face is filled with light. It dances over his cheeks and eyelashes like gold dust sparkling in the sun. Next to him, Dar creeps along the ground to tangle with his shadow. All I had before meeting Lucas and his family was darkness; I never knew how much I also craved the light. It gives a sharper shape to my shadows. I need them both.

Shadows alone are no longer enough.

I watch Lucas's light shift from the usual band into something different this time: a thin golden coil of rope, twisting in the air before us. I clap my hands, and he opens his eyes wide.

"I did it!" he says, laughing. When he reaches out, the rope gives resistance, and he lets out a whoop. He grabs my hand and swings me around in a circle, the rope dangling in the air between us. I throw my head back and laugh with him, filled with light and shadow and hope.

Now that Lucas's attention has strayed, his rope doesn't last for long, dissolving into the sunbeams. But it's a start. A very good start indeed.

←—•—→

We spend most of the afternoon working on our talents together, and Lucas makes great progress in making his light more tangible. The sun is almost all the way across the sky when Miranda ventures out to pick vegetables for dinner. She smiles when she sees us using our talents together. I've remade my shadow gazebo from earlier, and Lucas has draped gleaming ropes of light around the edges.

"I see you two are getting along quite famously," she says. "At least some of us are having a good day. Your father has spent the whole afternoon wearing out the floorboards in his study."

She kneels by the garden and sighs, bracing herself momentarily on one of the planks edging the vegetable patch. Lucas hurries over.

"What's wrong, Mum?" he asks, frowning.

She gives him a halfhearted smile and brushes a lock of his hair out of his eyes. "I'm fine, dear. Just woke up with a headache this morning. Been getting worse all day. But I'm sure it will pass after a good night's sleep."

"We can help you pick the vegetables, can't we, Emmeline?" Lucas says as I join them.

"Of course," I say. Up close, Miranda's face looks more drawn than usual with a new crease marring her brow.

I am almost surprised Dar has not made any snide remarks about Miranda. She has done so at every chance she gets lately.

With a start, I realize Dar is not here. She is not at my feet, and if I'm being honest, I've been so distracted by Lucas, I'm not sure how long she's been gone. All that remains is that string, thin as a whisper, tying us together. I bend down, pretending to tie my boot and give the line a sharp tug. If she was bored, she probably wandered off to play in the woods.

I frown when I see her familiar shape slide under the door

of the cottage. What was Dar doing inside the house? She does not offer an explanation, but she slinks over to me puffed out as though she's very pleased with herself. I find it oddly worrying.

We'll have to chat about this later tonight. It isn't safe for Dar to be going off on her own right now. And I can't help wondering what she was up to.

I kneel down next to Lucas to help him and Miranda fill the basket with carrots, green beans, and potatoes. I recall Dar's lack of a reaction to the dressmaker's shop so similar to the one she died in, and sneak another glance at my shadow. My circling thoughts nip at me, but I squash them down.

I must remain focused on our mission.

CHAPTER SIXTEEN

I have only been here for five days, but already I have grown accustomed to our daily ritual. During the day, Lucas and I do chores and then work with our crafts. He is a quick study and gets better at making his light tangible and tacky every day. At night, the family retreats to their beds, and I rest while Dar keeps watch. Every once in a while she's urged me to hide near the study to spy on Alfred and Miranda, but I've refused. While a piece of me is dying to know who Winthrop is and what plans he's a part of, the thought of eavesdropping again on these people who've shown me nothing but kindness and generosity makes my stomach turn. Eavesdropping has long been my way to learn about people who refused to talk to me, but I do not feel like I need it as much here.

Almost every night, when the shadows are deep enough and everyone else slumbers, Dar wakes me and we set about finding the next ingredient for the ritual. But tonight, I open my eyes and see the moon is high in the sky outside my window.

And Dar is nowhere in sight for the second time today. Only a thin shadowy line runs from the tip of my toe and under my door.

I jolt upright in my bed. "Dar!" I hiss.

A few tense moments later I see her silky form slide underneath my bedroom door and settle into her usual place. I frown.

"Where were you?"

I went to play with the shadows in the kitchen while I waited for you.

"But what about Miranda and Alfred? They didn't notice you before they retired, did they?"

Dar weaves over the floor as I stand up. *No*, she says. *They saw nothing at all.*

Something about the way she says it makes me nervous.

The last time she wandered off at night was the incident with Lord Tate, and something in her tone reminds me of that too.

But Miranda and Alfred and Lucas are our friends; Dar has no real cause to think I need protecting from them despite her suspicions. Even so, something tenses in my stomach and refuses to let go no matter how much I try to reason it away.

Tonight we're in search of three white candles. Now that the new dress Miranda arranged for me has arrived, I'm careful to wear one of her old shifts on this late night excursion just in case I have to go somewhere muddy again. I creep from my guest room to search the kitchen cabinets, hopeful that this will be a relatively easy task. I'd much rather borrow them from Lucas's family than steal from someone else. When I triumphantly pull a box of candles from a drawer, Dar withers.

Those are yellow. They must be white.

My bubble of hope deflates. I hunt through every nook and cranny I can find, but there are no white candles in the entire house.

I sigh, and slip from the cottage to dodge through the shadows in the woods.

Let's try the village, Dar suggests.

"But I don't have any money to buy them," I say. Yet another thing I should have brought with me in my flight and completely forgot.

That won't matter.

"What do you mean?" I frown.

You shall see.

She doesn't explain herself further. I do not like it when my shadow keeps secrets from me. This makes two in one night. I shiver.

But there is little else I can do but follow her lead. My feet know the path to the village better than they should. Even the trees have gotten used to us passing by, and they bend the shadows of their branches toward us in what feels like casual familiarity. Shadows join us, winding through my legs, but I don't feel elation this time. Tonight, I just want this task to be done. This will be the third night we have snuck out of the house. Many nights staying up late have left me exhausted. It is starting to show in the circles under my eyes and the drag in my steps.

Lucas and his family will notice soon if they haven't already. And that will raise questions I cannot answer. Not yet.

The orchard surrounding the village comes into view, the apple trees throwing their gnarled shadows into the fray that escorts us. The village doesn't have much to guard it. There is no fence, no wall like there is around my parents' estate. Here a few paths from different directions lead past a smattering of buildings, which grow tighter the farther into the village we go. I wrap my shadows around me, walking down the center of the main thoroughfare and turning when Dar directs.

By the time she stops me I am so disoriented, I'm not even sure if I'm in the same village any longer. Before me stands a simple building of white sandstone, but on closer examination is revealed to be something more. The lower level windows are filled with multicolored glass arranged into the shape of a star shooting across a night sky. This must be a temple to the Cerelia Comet. I have heard of them in my books, but never seen one before. Legend tells that the first time the comet flew over our lands, it sprinkled the ground with the first seeds of life, bringing blessings anew every twenty-five years. Many people revere the comet to this day and build beautiful temples like this one.

This place should have the white candles we need.

But something about the building stops me. It seems peaceful and simply perfect. I can't quite bring myself to disturb its slumber. After all, the comet did bless me with my talent.

"Isn't there some other place? Some other way?"

Dar sighs. *No, there is not. We are staying in the middle of the woods. We have to use what we can find. And this is close.*

I snort. "I don't call a mile walk in the middle of the night close." Dar's form folds into a smile.

I take a hesitant step on the cobbled path leading to the door. "Should I wake someone up to ask for the candles?"

Dar glows a filmy red. *So many questions. These days you seem to trust Lucas more than me.*

The hint of venom in her voice is jolting. She must be feeling neglected lately. I was afraid of that. I brush my fingertips over her edges. "Don't worry, you're a part of me. I'll always trust you. I just don't understand what I need to do here."

Duck inside and take the candles on the altar.

"Take them?" I balk. Stealing from a temple to the Cerelia Comet feels like a betrayal of sorts.

Dar sighs again. *They aren't just going to give them to you, and we have no money, do we? What did you expect?*

"I just—I don't like the idea of stealing."

Don't think of it as stealing. It's for a good purpose, isn't it? Something that will help you and me and that man in a coma at your parents' estate. Or have you forgotten him already?

A vise forms around my chest. I know—*I know*—that Dar is correct.

Unless of course you don't want to set things right…

My spine straightens, and I shove down the sick feeling in my gut. It has gotten steadily worse since I woke up to find Dar missing earlier. I have to do this, no matter how much my conscience screams at me.

With my shadows surrounding me, I open the gate in front of the temple and walk down the little stone pathway. The front door is unlocked and opens easily. I duck into the nearest corner and hold my breath. My heart hammers in my ears.

But no one comes running, no one comes out with accusing fingers that can pierce through to my heart. No one appears at all.

The inside of the temple is lovely. Whitewashed walls and stained-glass windows reflect the moonlight on the stone floor, well-worn from years of use. At the front of the temple lies an altar lined with white candles, some lit, some not, some beginning to sputter out, that make the whole room seem to glow. For a second, I imagine what Lucas would do with that light if he were here. He'd probably make the candlelight dance and swirl around the temple, maybe combining with the stained glass windows for some lovely effect. Dar, on the other hand, would surely be happier if we snuffed them all out.

An ache builds in my chest. What would Lucas think if he could see me now?

I will my feet to inch closer to the altar. When I reach it, my hands hover over the array. There are so many candles.

If you check under the altar, there may be extras. Take three of those; no one will notice.

A crate of newly-fashioned white candles rests under the drapings of the altar. I tuck three into my skirt pockets, swallowing my bitter guilt in the process.

This place is beautiful, especially here at night in the darkness, but I want nothing more than to leave it as soon as possible.

Perfect, Dar purrs. I can feel the warmth of her smile at my back as I flee the temple, less careful than when I came inside. Soon I run through the village, shadows secured around me, trying to get far away from the things I've done in the name of friendship.

CHAPTER SEVENTEEN

The next evening, when dusk has fallen and Lucas and I are playing with the shadows in the yard, hoofbeats resound through the woods. Fear bites into me, and I grab Lucas's hand, yanking him down behind the vegetable garden and wrapping my shadows around us. We huddle together, wide-eyed and waiting. The memory of the soldiers at the front door and in the village is all too fresh.

It's all right, you're safe here in the darkness with me, Dar says in my ear.

"Who do you think it is?" My heart gallops in my chest, like it is racing the riders to the cottage door.

Lucas peers into the dark woods, but he can't see much.

"I'm not sure. But Mum did mention that some friends of ours might visit soon. Maybe it's them?"

I relax my grip on his arm—slightly. "Bad day for it though," I say. Miranda has been complaining of a headache again. Something about nightmares and not sleeping well. I glance at Dar, hoping for the hundredth time today that it had nothing to do with her sneaking off last night.

Lucas reaches out a hand through my shadowcraft just to see it shrouded in darkness. He pulls it back, wonder written on his face.

"They really won't be able to see us?"

I shake my head. "Not even a little."

"I wish I could conceal myself with my light singing. All I do is blind people on occasion."

I stifle a laugh, but my smile still squeaks out. "Your light is wonderful. And you're getting better with it every day." The hoofbeats grow louder, but Lucas has softened the edges of my fear. A few moments later, four riders—two adults, and two children on ponies behind them—come to a halt in Lucas's yard. His face lights up.

"It *is* our friends after all! Come on, Emmeline, you must

meet them." He leaps to his feet and runs toward the newcomers, while I cautiously dissipate my shadows.

Careful, Dar warns. *You don't know if you can trust them. Don't let them see what you can do. The last thing we need is more people knowing about your talent.*

"If they're friends of Lucas, they must be trustworthy," I whisper.

Dar growls. *Lucas doesn't know everything. He could be wrong. Together, you and I have excellent judgment. We should decide for ourselves.*

"Don't worry, I'll be careful. See? I'm letting the shadows go slowly. They'll never know." She has been having outbursts like this more often lately. Hopefully, once the ritual is complete, she will be back to normal again.

Dar quiets as I approach Lucas and his friends. The father and mother both have dark hair and deeply tanned skin with smiles that brighten the night as much as Lucas and his light. They are laughing at something Lucas has told them.

"Emmeline, this the Rodan family. Mr. and Mrs. Rodan, and Cary"—Lucas points to the girl—"and Doyle," he finishes, pointing to the boy who seems to be about our age. The girl is older and taller than her brother, and looks like a smaller version of her mother. Her eyes are the same fierce blue, striking against the rest of her dusky features. Her brother has dark eyes and a snub nose, and the wind seems to be constantly blowing through his hair, making it stand on end.

"It is nice to meet you," I say. My hands itch to make something, to give them a little shadow gift, but I'm too wary for that.

"There you are!" Miranda calls from the doorway. "Come in, come in, there's water and shelter for your horses behind the cottage." She smiles warmly, but dark circles frame her eyes.

Mr. Rodan leads the horses away, while the others follow us inside. Fireflies dance in my stomach. I am not at home here, but I've just begun to feel at ease around Lucas and his parents. What if these newcomers don't like me? Will I be sent away? My throat suddenly feels thick.

I don't want to leave here. I want to stay and play in the woods with Lucas and learn about his light singing.

Miranda guides us to the sitting room, and we settle onto the couches and chairs. A sudden need to be close to Lucas's light twinges in my chest, and I sit beside him.

Dar sniffs in my ear. *I don't know about these people. They're too friendly. Only liars are that happy.*

I must talk to Dar about her suspicions of everyone, but I tuck that thought away for later. I know she only wants to protect me, but sometimes she goes too far.

The way these people talk and laugh easily with each other is entrancing. From their conversation, I gather it has been months since they have been together, but the connections between them are so clear and strong that I can almost see them. There is no hint of jealousy or petulance, not like there always seems to be lately with Dar.

My limbs begin to tingle. I want this—friendship and laughter and no fear of using magic.

I'm lost in my thoughts, and Dar's voice startles me. *When I am whole again, we'll be able to talk and laugh and play like that too. Everything will be so much better then. It will be just you and me. We won't need anyone else.*

My shadow pools at my side, playing along and acting like a normal shadow today, but her words trouble me. I can't help thinking that if Lucas knew about Dar, he wouldn't insist on leaving her behind like she wants me to leave him; he'd welcome and include her. Still, a happy Dar is better than a jealous Dar. I smile and reach down for a moment, grazing the edges of her form, so she knows I heard her and look forward to it too.

"Emmeline," Lucas says, diverting my attention. "You must see what Doyle can do." He grins, but the Rodans' smiles falter.

Lucas's mother sighs. "It's all right. Emmeline has a talent too."

My heart leaps into my throat. "I—I—"

See? Dar wails in my ears. *I told you they could not be trusted with your secret!*

Lucas puts a warm hand on my arm. I stare at it. "Don't worry, we can trust them. I promise. Watch."

Doyle slides off his chair with a sly grin on his face. He puts two fingers between his teeth and makes a sharp, bright noise. Seconds later, the curtains by the windows billow into the room, and the front door clangs open, making me jump. Lucas laughs, and my eyes widen at the sight before me.

The boy throws his arms up as the wind whirls around him in a churning column. Papers fly and leaves from outside are caught up by it. The wind forms a spinning ball in front of him, then he hurls it toward the cottage door. It flies back outside, the door slamming shut behind it.

I clap and laugh despite my initial terror. "What a wonderful talent!" I say.

That explains why his hair is a little mussed, like the wind has just blown through it.

Doyle does a little bow, and climbs back on his chair. I'm dying to know what else he can do with his wind whistling, but his sister, Cary, yawns as though she has seen this trick a hundred times. She probably has. Suddenly her eyes light up.

"Lucas, do you have any new tricks? Or your friend maybe?"

Lucas, seeing my hesitation, stands up. "Of course." Without further ado, he begins to sing, and the light from the candles in the cottage snap off their wicks and float through the air toward him. They spin in a circle over his head, moving faster and faster until he's surrounded by a golden halo. Cary grins and claps as he finishes his song. On the last note, he sends the light back to their candles, where they stand as though nothing happened at all.

Show off, Dar mutters. *Your shadows are far better crafted.*

Expectant silence fills the room, with all eyes fixed on me. I want to wrap my shadows around me and hide, but I stamp down that instinct.

"You don't have to show them now if you don't want to, dear," Miranda says. "Magic is a personal thing."

"And for good reason," Mrs. Rodan says. "You're right to hesitate before showing off to strangers." She shoots a meaningful glance at her son. "Your instincts will serve you well."

Lucas smiles encouragingly at me, but his mother clears her throat. "It's late, and I think we've all had enough excitement for this evening. It is time for the children to go to bed." She stands. "Come on, Doyle, Cary, we've got extra cots for you both. Cary, you'll be in the same room as Emmeline, and Doyle, you'll bunk with Lucas."

I trail after them like a shadow myself, but when Lucas looks back at me and beams, light fills me from my head to my toes.

←———→

I lay on my cot, Dar at my side, a few feet away from Cary. She didn't say much other than "I bet your magic is more fun than my brother's" and "good night," before she turned on her side and began to snore.

This is the time of night when Dar and I usually set out to collect an item for the ritual, but with the guests here—still awake and chatting in the sitting room—I don't know if I should risk it. I never worried my parents might check on me when I was at home. But what if Mrs. Rodan checked on Cary and noticed I was missing? Then I'd have to answer for what I was doing in the woods at such a late hour. I don't know how many times I can use the sleepwalking excuse and get away with it.

Dar spills across my pillow. *If they don't stop jabbering soon, we shall have to wait until they leave. The full blood moon approaches swiftly so we can't afford many delays, but it's too risky tonight with everyone awake still.*

"I don't know how long they're staying," I whisper.

Hopefully not long, Dar says sharply. I curl onto my side.

"Don't be upset. I like them, but you're my best friend. No one can take your place."

She wiggles. *I am sorry. I hate being locked up like this. I want to play in the darkness.*

"Soon," I promise. I lay on my back, but try as I might I still cannot fall asleep. The soft murmur of the adults' voices echoes down the hallway.

A wicked idea blooms in my mind.

"Dar, how would you like to have a little fun right now?"

She perks up, billowing out. *I'm all ears.*

I swing my legs over the side of the bed and my bare feet hit the cold floor. Mrs. Rodan's words from earlier about my instincts serving me well have been niggling at me. "I want to know what they talk about. Maybe they're here for a reason, not just a visit."

Dar grows darker, her eagerness becoming a palpable thing.

I gather my shadows to me as quietly as I can, so not to wake Cary. She doesn't stir, and by the time I'm fully covered, my boldness has returned. I crack the door open, and the voices of the adults grow louder. There hasn't been much laughter, not like there was earlier or before they arrived.

They must be discussing something serious.

Curiosity tingles up my arms, and I keep my shadows close as I creep down the hall. No one will see me unless I let them.

I tiptoe to the edge of the sitting room but remain hidden in the shadows.

I've missed this, Dar murmurs, and I can't help but agree. Listening in on people—my parents, the odd visitor, the cook—always gave me a thrill. It made me feel closer to them, as if I actually knew them. Though tonight it's tinged with an undercurrent of guilt.

"Stay as long as you need to," Miranda says.

"Thank you, but it will be a brief visit this time," Mr. Rodan says. "Only a day or two at most."

"That is likely safest. If Lady Aisling suspects you were hiding in Parilla, then moving on to Abbacho as quickly as possible is for the best," Alfred says.

My body goes rigid. Tate and his companion spoke of Lady Aisling, too. Tate *worked* for her.

That can't be good, Dar says, a tremor in her voice.

This time, I dare to peer around the corner to see them. The adults sit on opposite sides of the couch, while Lucas's father refills their glasses with a light, sparkling liquid.

Miranda is oddly quiet and stares at her glass as the liquid swirls inside it. Alfred puts a hand on her shoulder. "Don't worry, she has no reason to stop here. No one even knows this cottage exists."

Mrs. Rodan sighs. "We should have followed your lead and moved every two years to a different spot in the woods. It was smart of you. And it was foolish of us not to take advantage of the network sooner." She lowers her voice and sets her glass on the table untouched as though she can't stomach it anymore. "Did you hear about the Hamlins' daughter? Lady Aisling got her claws into her a few weeks ago. Her soldiers have been prowling villages on the border of Zinnia and Parilla for more talented children ever since, and are moving steadily inward. Their cover has something to do with that treaty the Zinnians proposed to unite all three territories under one rule."

The hair raises on the back of my neck, shooting shivers down my spine. This Lady Aisling is looking for talented children? I knew she and Tate offered a cure to those parents who had problems with their children's talents, but actively hunting for them is another matter entirely. It seems Lord Tate was not really visiting my parents' estate about a treaty after all.

I told you Tate was no good, Dar mutters.

"That's why we decided it was time for a change of scenery," Mr. Rodan says.

Miranda manages a weak smile. "Well, I hear Abbacho is lovely this time of year."

They laugh, but even that can't release the undercurrent of tension strung through the four of them like a bow.

"We have your papers for you," Miranda says, shuffling something on a table. "And just last week our friends at the network informed us that your residence is ready. Lady Aisling will not be able to find you easily."

Mr. Rodan sighs. "Yes, as long as the Abbachon nobles don't ever sign that treaty."

My head reels with the implications. What is the network that they speak of? Was this missing Winthrop involved with the network too? Miranda said he was a flame breather, but surely he was too old for Lady Aisling. And he wasn't a child in need of a cure.

Dar winds her silky fingers through my hair. *Don't worry, Lady Aisling won't get you. I promise you that. We'll flee at the first sign of danger.*

"But what about Lucas and his family?" I whisper.

Dar sighs. *They can come too. If they must.*

Miranda picks up the empty glasses on the table and moves toward the kitchen—and the hallway where I hide. I suck my breath in sharply and flatten myself in the shadows in my corner. She passes within inches of me and doesn't bat an eye. I don't dare move. I have to pass by the kitchen doorway to get back to my room. When she returns to the sitting room a few minutes later without incident I finally breathe out again.

That was too close. My estate was spacious and had many more corners to hide in, making eavesdropping easy. The cottage is much smaller and hiding is more of a challenge. I shouldn't take a risk like this again.

The adults change topics, something about trade and life in the woods. I tiptoe back to the guest room and slip inside. When my head hits the pillow, I set my shadows free and let troubled dreams wash over me.

CHAPTER EIGHTEEN

The next morning, I wake to find Cary's cot empty. I dress quickly while Dar yawns at my feet, then hurry into the kitchen. After what I overheard last night, I don't want to miss anything from these visitors, even if they are delaying our plans to perform Dar's ritual.

But when I get there, I notice that Lucas's face is darker than usual today. In fact, he looks like he hasn't slept at all. I catch the tail end of Miranda's words to her son from the doorway.

"…we all get them sometimes, dear. But the good news is, nightmares aren't real, and we don't have to carry them with us in the light of day." She ruffles his hair, but his face is still drawn.

First Miranda, now Lucas? I can't help thinking again of Lord Tate and what happened to him over one night. I don't want to believe that Dar had a hand in this, but what exactly does she do while I sleep? I eye her warily, but my shadow gives no indication that anything is amiss.

I slip into a chair at the table and it isn't until I've reached for a roll that Doyle notices me.

"When did you get up?" he says, narrowing his eyes.

"A few minutes ago," I say, slathering some butter on my breakfast.

"Well, you sure are quiet," he says.

Lucas laughs, but it doesn't quite reach his eyes today. "It's her talent." He glances at me uncertainly. "Do you mind telling them what it is? You don't have to show them if you don't want to."

My mouth goes dry. This shouldn't be such a hurdle for me. But after Mother and Father treating it like an embarrassment and going so far as to try to send me away because of it, I can't help but hesitate.

I swallow hard. "I'm a shadow weaver."

Cary's eyes light up. "Really? What can you do with shadows? They always seem to be stuck to walls and floors."

A smile creeps over my face. "Not for me."

"She can make stuff from them," Lucas says.

"You must show us!" Doyle says, accidentally spitting crumbs from the roll he is eating across the table.

"Doyle, don't talk with your mouth full. It's rude." Cary hands him a napkin and rolls her eyes. "Sorry, but it does sound intriguing. We'd love to see it, if you don't mind sharing."

Dar sniffs at my feet. *Show them, then I can play with the shadows for a while without anyone catching on. I long to have some fun. I never get to have fun anymore.*

The edge in her voice concerns me, but I put that aside for now.

"All right, I'll show you." I pop the last bit of roll in my mouth, and before I can even swallow, Lucas grabs my hand and tugs me toward the front door. His energy seems to be coming back.

"I have a great idea—let's go outside, and we can show them how my light singing and your shadow weaving work together!" Lucas says.

It is sunnier than I usually prefer when I play but being in the middle of the woods makes up for it. I call the shadows of the trees at the edge of the yard, pulling them closer with my hands, then weaving them into a giant ball. I let it dip close to the ground, and Dar slips in unnoticed. Then it spins and spins, puffing out more and more, faster and faster, until it surrounds all four of us. Inside the giant shadow ball, the sunlight is only a hazy memory over our heads. It seems as though night has set when the day has hardly begun.

It's lovely. I missed our outing last night more than I'd realized. Being surrounded by shadows is something I've grown accustomed to all these years, so being without or having fewer feels strange.

Cary and Doyle gasp. "This is incredible!" Doyle says.

"It's better than your stupid wind," his sister says.

He scowls and shoves her in the arm, but she just smirks.

"Thank you," I say, feeling rather pleased with my work. It isn't even the most remarkable thing I've crafted, but it's large enough to impress these new friends.

Dar cackles in my ear. *His sister is right. His wind whistling is unimpressive next to your shadow weaving.*

At my side, Lucas begins to sing, the notes leaving his mouth as tiny specks of light. They swoop and soar through the darkness of the yard, teasing my hair and making me laugh. He sends them diving toward Doyle—who ducks—then settles them over our heads, like little stars.

I clap along, caught up in the magic as much as the others. A light breeze wanders through the air, and I wonder if it's Doyle, perhaps feeling a little left out.

This, right here, this is peaceful. I feel free and happy and accepted by every person here. No one lies to my face or pretends to like me just to please my parents. They don't even know who my parents are.

They're my friends.

It fills me up inside with some strange, unnameable thing. I feel lighter than I ever have before, like I could take on anything or run a hundred miles. This is what it will be like when Dar is human again. She won't be sullen and jealous anymore, and she'll only add to this joy. And I'll never have to let it go.

←—•—→

We play outside for most of the day, pausing only for lunch. It has been a few days since we last saw the guards, so the adults don't object to us playing in the woods now. We wander down to a nearby pond where Lucas baits fish with his light, and Doyle swoops them out of the water with his wind. But by the time we return to the cottage, the sun is going down.

Miranda calls to us as soon as she sees us. "We're waiting for you to eat dinner. Come in, please!"

"Just a few more minutes, Mum? I want to show them how I can make things grow at night," Lucas asks his mother, but she shakes her head.

"Dinner, Lucas. Now."

"Fine." He scowls, unconsciously bending the light around him into daggers wherever he looks.

"You won't want to miss dinner with the Rodans. They're only here for another day or two. Take advantage of it."

"They're leaving so soon? But why?" Lucas asks. Doyle fidgets next to him.

Miranda puts a hand on Lucas's shoulder and leads him toward the house. "It's the safest thing for them to do. For all of us. They can't stay here for long. The night after tomorrow, they'll be heading out again. We'll just have to enjoy the time while they're here."

Good riddance, Dar mutters, and my cheeks turn pink. For once I'm glad that I'm the only one who can hear Dar.

"Are you going to start moving around a lot like we do?" Lucas asks Cary and Doyle.

"Maybe," Cary says, the expression on her face unreadable.

"That's too bad. I liked your house in Parilla," Lucas says. He turns to his mother. "And I liked our last cottage in Abbacho better than this one too."

"I know, Lucas, but it's more important that we be safe," Miranda says.

He kicks a loose pebble as we enter the house. I follow them like a shadow, the curiosity inside my chest turning my expression into a question. One that Lucas's mother recognizes when she glances back at me.

She sighs. "You're wondering why we move around so much, aren't you, Emmeline?"

"It does seem a bit unusual," I say. "And this is such a lovely cottage. It would be sad to leave it behind in a year or two."

"Not as sad as being discovered by Lady Aisling," Lucas's father says, giving his wife a kiss on the cheek. He sobers when he sees the expression on my face. "You don't know about Lady Aisling, do you?"

I shake my head. "I've heard the name, but that's all."

Miranda's face pales. "You must be careful. We assumed she was the reason you hid your talent. Come, we'll explain over dinner."

They usher us toward the kitchen table, and Lucas helps his mother set the food out for us all to share. We join the Rodans and load up our plates, while I try not to burst with curiosity. I wish Dar was talking. She knows much more than I do about Zinnia and Lady Aisling, but she has gone into a silent sulk under the table. Maybe she wants to listen to what they have to say too.

Lucas digs into his meal, but the adults push their food around their plates. Miranda finally puts her fork down.

"Emmeline, do you know how people like you and Lucas obtained their magic?"

I nod. "Yes, every twenty-five years the Cerelia Comet sails by, blessing a few pregnant mothers in its wake with children with magical abilities."

"That's right. Now you've heard of Zinnia, yes?"

Heat slides down my spine. That is where Tate wanted to take me. "It's the territory on the other side of Parilla."

"Indeed it is. But you really haven't heard of Lady Aisling?"

Dar rears up from the floor, and wraps around my knees. *Don't tell them about what happened to me yet. Let's see how much they know first.*

My heart clenches at my shadow's plea. "The name is familiar, but I don't know much about who she is," I say. Dar relaxes her grip on my knees.

Lucas's parents and the Rodans share a knowing frown. "Well, you should," Alfred says. "She's the leading noble of the territory, famous for the grand parties she throws in her Garden of Souls, but she's dangerous for people like you, Lucas, and Doyle."

The image of Simone's ghostly face flashes in front of my eyes and makes my hands tremble.

Miranda downs half of her water glass in one gulp. "Lady Aisling collects talented children like yourselves. She and her emissaries scour the countryside for them, then trick their parents with promises of a cure."

My spine straightens, and I try not to show my reaction,

but my hands twist in my skirts. This sounds all too familiar, and I fear my galloping heart will give me away.

Lucas's father scoffs. "There is no cure, of course. It is merely a ruse to convince the parents to send their children away to Zinnia."

My brow furrows. "But what is she doing with them?" I can almost feel the cold grazing of Simone's eyes.

"No one knows for certain, though there are many theories. Some believe she's training them to be her personal army."

"Maybe she needs them to tend to her giant garden," Doyle suggests through a mouthful of food.

"I think Lady Aisling is stealing their magic somehow," Cary says.

Lucas swallows a huge bite of toast. "But who could do that? And how?"

I shudder and stare at my plate. My appetite has all but vanished. Deep in my bones I know with utter certainty that is exactly what she is doing. Simone was so damaged… Something awful must have happened to her.

Something Lady Aisling did. She may have a garden full of beautiful flowers, but her heart is a wretched, cruel thing.

"That's terrible," I say, trying not to let my fear show. I bite my lip to keep it from trembling.

"Maybe that is it, Cary," Miranda says. "But the trouble is no one knows because no one sees the children again." She doesn't mention the adults that have been going missing, but I recall her words from the other night about Winthrop. This is bigger than she is letting on. She probably doesn't want to scare us any more than necessary.

A silence falls over the table, broken only by Lucas slurping a green bean. His mother tousles his curls.

"We used to live near Zinnia, right on the border of Parilla," Alfred says. "Lucas was only a year old when a neighbor child around the same age was taken away by soldiers and a strange, frightful woman. The child's parents barely remembered that they had ever had a baby at all. Lady Aisling did something to them, I'd stake my life on it. Not long after, we began to notice how Lucas could bend the light around him."

Miranda sets her napkin down. "We knew what it meant, and we left for the forest as soon as possible to protect him from Lady Aisling."

My thoughts swirl through my head, many of them

falling into place clearly. Winthrop is one of the missing talented people, though he's older which seems strange. And this network they mentioned, it must have something to do with hiding people from Lady Aisling. Miranda and Alfred are clearly more involved then they're letting on, if they're relaying messages from the mysterious network to the Rodans.

They're out here in the woods hiding from Lady Aisling and helping others move around to evade capture. That's why they were so disturbed by the guards. The list I found is still a mystery, though I'm willing to bet it's related in some way too.

Words bubble up in my throat. But before I can let them out, Dar squeals from behind my chair. *Please, protect me, just until we perform the ritual. I can protect you from Lady Aisling. I know what that wicked woman wants: lost souls, just like me. She is the reason I became one in the first place. Please, I can't risk being recaptured. Don't admit what you know.*

I rest a hand on Dar's form still wrapped around the back of my chair and give it a squeeze. She relaxes, but my stomach is more in knots than ever before. She told me Lady Aisling was a stranger, a noble who caused an accident in a seamstress shop. If that's the case, why is she so afraid of her now? Why would she fear being captured?

I may live in shadows, but I fear I am more in the dark about Dar than I ever suspected. I hate to admit it, but between the lying, the stealing, the sneaking, and now this, it is becoming difficult to trust her. We are going to have to have a long talk as soon as the Rodans are gone.

I may not tell my new friends about Dar and what I know of Lady Aisling yet, but once this ritual is over and things are set right, I will tell them everything.

CHAPTER NINETEEN

I have been doing my best to ignore Dar's strange behavior, but I caught her sneaking back into my bedroom this morning when she thought I was still asleep. She always has an easy answer ready—too easy. Something is wrong. I just want to get the ritual over with so that I can get my friend back. I know the ritual is the key to fixing everything.

But despite the rocky start, the morning is full of promise and laughter as we sit around the kitchen table, watching Lucas practice his baking by toasting croissants and browning sausages for our amusement and breakfast. Yesterday, he made Cary, Doyle, and me night-lights—glowing orbs that he captured in a bottle. Now there are several of them strung throughout the house. He seems determined to keep light from ever leaving him.

I can't blame him; it's a beautiful golden color, but it shines a bit too brightly for me. Though it does remind me of the jar of shadows and fireflies I made for Kendra once. I know Lucas would've appreciated a gift like that. He's a true friend. The bottle of light now rests in my flour sack stowed under my cot. Cary hasn't noticed the sack yet, and with any luck, she never will. The shadow I've placed over it like a blanket doesn't hurt either. She doesn't seem a prying sort, though her brother is another matter.

"What else can you do with shadows, Emmeline?" Doyle scrunches up his nose from across the table. "Anything practical like Lucas?"

Dar bristles under my feet, and I feel it tingling in my toes. I must figure out how to keep her under better control until we complete the ritual. "If you mean can I cook with shadows, then no, I'm afraid not. But shadows can be useful in other ways. I can make a kite, or a cloak." I pause remembering the bridge I made to get away from the soldiers when I first fled my home. "And things like rope too. I made a shadow bridge once."

Doyle frowns and Cary laughs. "Were you able to walk on it? Did it hold?"

I smile. "It did."

Lucas sits down, tossing a few sausages and two croissants on his plate. "Emmeline has been helping me make my light more tangible, like she can with shadows."

"Do you think that could work with wind?" Doyle asks.

I shrug. "I don't know. I've never seen anyone try. But if it works with shadow and light, I don't see why it wouldn't work for wind."

Doyle breaks into a grin and says, "Let's try it after breakfast."

Dar moans at my feet. *Not the wind whistler too. The light singing is bad enough, but wind whistling is a truly useless talent.*

I laugh, ignoring Dar's objections. "All right."

We eat quickly, then dash outside. I show them something simple at first, how I can make a shadow into a rope, while Lucas works on a band of light that curls around his wrist. I focus on crafting the shadow into something real, something that can be felt, and soon the shadow rope lays in my hands. I hold it out, then direct it to soar toward Doyle. He laughs as it chases him across the yard. Then it catches him, winding around his body and pinning his arms to his sides. Cary is delighted by this and laughs so hard I fear she might burst. Dar, too, cackles at my side. Doyle scowls, then whistles loudly. Wind whips through the trees, tugging at the shadow rope until it finally releases its hold on him.

"I wish I could do that to him when he gets on my nerves," Cary says wistfully.

"Very funny," Doyle says pouting, then scuffing his toe on the ground. "But that was really neat. How did you do it?"

"It takes a lot of concentration. You have to focus on expanding the mass."

Doyle furrows his brow and whistles. His wind flies to him, but even I can tell his control of his talent is not yet as sophisticated as mine or Lucas's. But still he tries and tries and tries again.

Lucas and I help, giving him encouragement and tips, but after an hour we have to admit it is to no avail. Cary is the only one relieved. Her expression soured as the minutes ticked by. I have to wonder what it's like to have a brother blessed with a talent and no talent of your own. I always wished I had a sibling, but watching the two of them interact, I think it is better that I have Dar instead. Cary is protective and bored by Doyle at the same time. Or perhaps that is how all siblings are. Dar and I have a bond that is unbreakable. I only hope it will last after the ritual is complete.

The shadows deepen in the guest room I share with Cary, and once I hear her snoring, I rise at Dar's behest.

We only need a couple more items for the ritual, then we're done, Dar says, her voice threaded with excitement. Her form is edged in silver tonight, something I've never seen before. She's never been so excited, not even for our best tricks and games over the years. I am relieved to see her in good spirits for the first time in days.

I lace up my boots as quietly as I can, listening for any hint that Cary wakes. Then I tiptoe from the room, weighed down by the heavy flour sack in my hand. "I thought you had wanted to wait until the Rodans were gone?"

We can't afford to wait any longer, not if they plan to

stay for another couple days. The blood moon will have passed by then.

"What must we get? Is it far this time?"

Not at all. Outside, Dar says. *To the garden.*

I slink out the back door, fully cloaked in shadows. An uneasy feeling makes me pause as the door closes behind me. I peer at the woods, but I don't see anything. Far off in the forest, something howls, and I shiver.

It must be the animals nearby making me nervous. Though they never have before. Usually the dark is a comfort.

The garden is close to the house, and I reach it quickly. The vegetables' leaves seem silver in the moonlight, but most of the flowers are squeezed shut. At the far end of the garden is Miranda's favorite plant: her rosebushes.

Dar nudges me toward the roses. *Take one. Break it off; then we're almost done. There will only be one more ingredient to collect.*

"Just one? That's all?" Relief rises in my chest in a warm steady stream. "Can we retrieve it now and perform the ritual tonight?"

We must wait until tomorrow night for the blood moon.

But we are so close. She curls around me, and I can feel her excitement vibrating through her misty form. It's mirrored in my own heart, success so close I can nearly reach out and grab it.

I pluck one of the roses from the back of the bush, stem and all, narrowly avoiding pricking my thumb on the thorns. I carefully place it in my flour sack but pause before I've taken more than a couple steps.

A new sound comes from the woods. Somewhere out there, maybe as close as Lucas's favorite field, a horse whinnies.

Every nerve in my body stands on end as the horses in the small barn behind the cottage whinny back.

Wait here, I'll check the woods as far as I can.

Dar glides along the ground, stretching her form into the forest and reaching out in both directions to cover more ground. I remind myself that she'll come back. She always does. I know she will even when she's in her human form again.

Every second panic builds in my chest. Finally, Dar returns to my side.

Go inside right now. We need to borrow Miranda's mortar and pestle and a small bottle, and then we need to leave.

I frown. "What? Why do we need to leave?"

There is no time to explain. Go to the kitchen, Emmeline. Hurry.

"Are we in danger?" I ask, trembling.

But *Hurry!* is all the answer Dar will give me.

I sneak into the kitchen and quietly rummage through the cabinets, praying I don't wake anyone up.

"Couldn't we ask her for them?"

And tell her what, exactly, when she wants to know why we need them?

My heart sinks. I can't ask to borrow anything without an explanation.

Finally, I find the items I need, a small glass bottle and the mortar and pestle Miranda uses to crush herbs. My hand pauses over the latter. I've seen her use this every day since I arrived. She needs it, but tonight I need it more. I hope she forgives me. I tuck it in my sack with a bitter taste on my tongue.

"Now what?"

We need to leave this place right now. The guards have found us. They're in the woods and getting closer every second.

Alarm pins my feet to the floor. "What? Why didn't you tell me this right away?" I lower my voice to a whisper. "How many? Is there any way through?"

North.

I check that my shadows are secure and tighten my grip on the flour sack of ingredients, then take one step toward the door before pausing. "I must warn the others. Lucas and Doyle are at risk too."

No! Dar cries. *Save yourself! Save me! They can fend for themselves. We don't have time!*

I consider it for a flash of a moment: leaving Lucas—kind, trusting Lucas—and his family and friends behind to fend for themselves against the guards who have been hunting for me all week.

This is what Dar wants. For me to leave them all behind for her. That's why she didn't tell me at first.

But it wouldn't be right. The guards wouldn't even be here if not for me and Dar.

"The guards work for Lady Aisling. I can't let Lucas and Doyle get caught."

I peek out the kitchen window. The silhouettes of the

soldiers in the woods now appear between the trees. Dar howls in my ears as I dash back into Lucas and Doyle's room.

Who cares if they get caught? All that matters is you and me. Leave now, Emmeline!

Dar's words chill me to the core, but I don't have time to chide her now.

"Get up!" I hiss, shaking Lucas. "Get up now!"

A groggy Lucas blinks at me. "Emmeline? What's going on?" he yawns.

"Lady Aisling's soldiers have the house surrounded. We have to leave right now."

Lucas's face turns green in the moonlight, but he bolts upright and pulls on his boots. I wake Doyle too and leave Lucas to explain before running into his parents' room. I feel rather naughty at barging into the adults' quarters but there is no help for it. I wake up Miranda first and at the words "Lady Aisling" she immediately reads the panic on my face and understands.

"Warn the Rodans."

I don't hesitate to obey. In only a handful of minutes we meet in the hall, Lucas and Doyle dragging a wide-eyed Cary with them.

"What direction are they coming from, Emmeline?" Miranda asks.

"Every direction. But there's thinner coverage to the north. Or at least there was a few minutes ago. If we leave now, we might still get past them."

Mr. Rodan speaks. "We'll get our horses and leave Doyle with you while we draw them off. We have no magic to steal; Lady Aisling can't hurt us if we're caught."

"And we'll sneak out through the root cellar to the north," Miranda says.

"We may not need to," I say. "I can hide the five of us in shadows while we sneak away under their noses. As long as we're quiet and watch where we step we should be fine. I've done it a hundred times on my own."

The adults give me a funny look, like they've swallowed something unpleasant. Inwardly I cringe, not sure what I said to make them react that way.

Before they can respond, something heavy smashes against the front door and soldiers pour into the house. I throw up my shadows, and the darkness surrounds us like a giant bubble. The Rodans race outside through the back door.

"Stay close to the wall," I whisper. "And don't say a word."

We inch toward the back door, keeping ourselves flat against the wall. Guards rush past us, not seeing us in the shadows. It feels a little different this time—and trickier—cloaking so many at once, but I keep my grasp on my shadows and they don't fail me.

Why didn't you just run, Emmeline? Dar moans. *Why would you choose these people over me? Over us?* I ignore her.

We hear shouts from outside as a few guards take off into the woods after the Rodans and their horses. But half remain here in the house, systematically searching every room and setting fire to it when they're done.

It's almost like they've been ordered to kill me if they can't capture me.

I shudder. Lucas takes my hand, offering silent comfort. My chest tightens. This is my fault. I don't deserve his comfort right now. But I squeeze back and don't let go. Dar grumbles in my ears.

The fire spreads outward like a drop in a pond, smoke billowing toward the ceiling in coiling waves. My breath hitches in my chest, and I struggle not to cough. The others face the same problem.

Flames begin to lick the beams over our heads, the awful creaking of the strained wood resounding in our ears.

The flames spit higher and we crouch close to the floor to avoid the smoke and the burning heat. If we don't escape soon, it will be too late and we'll definitely be discovered. Or worse.

The guards run from the house, like they've ceased their search and want to leave quickly. As soon as the last guard passes us, I gesture to the others and we hustle out the door unnoticed in the shadows.

The remaining soldiers stand back from the cottage near the tree line. We dash for the woods that aren't blocked in the opposite direction that the Rodans fled. None of us make a sound other than our ragged breathing and pounding hearts. When we reach the tree line, the moaning wood of the cottage collapses, and the fire flares up into the night.

We pause only for a moment, but the expressions on my friends' faces breaks my heart. The worst part is knowing I'm the one who put it there.

The soldiers stand watch, no doubt hoping someone will cry out for help in some hidden room. We hurry into the woods, letting the creaks and bursts from the cottage fire conceal our steps. Doyle stumbles over a fallen log, but bites his lip instead of crying out. His hands are covered in cuts and leaves, and tears shine in his eyes. Lucas's father lifts him up and sets the boy on his feet.

We push on, sometimes walking, sometimes running, for what seems like hours. I keep my shadows pulled tightly around us, but it is exhausting. My legs feel wobbly as a newborn colt's. Lucas puts a hand on my shoulder.

"Are you all right?" he whispers.

"I'm fine," I say breathlessly, then sink to my knees. Miranda helps me up.

"There's a cave not far ahead," she says. "We passed it when we moved to the cottage last year. We can camp there for the night. We could all use some sleep."

With her arm secured around my waist, I manage to make it to the cave. My hold on the shadows loosens, but they remain around us, wiggling and waiting for my command. As soon as we enter the cave I let them go, and they bound off through the woods to their homes.

Dizziness overtakes me, and someone sets me down,

resting my head on something soft. Comforting darkness closes in, but the guilt inside rears its head.

"I'm sorry," I murmur to the person next to me. "I'm so, so sorry."

CHAPTER TWENTY

When I wake, light streams in through the cave entrance, and several people stand near me in a circle, arguing. Somewhere nearby a fire crackles.

The blaze from last night at the cottage flares behind my eyes.

Mr. Rodan addresses Lucas's parents. "We can't take her with us. It's too risky. If she's being pursued by these soldiers, then she clearly lied about not knowing who Lady Aisling is. We can't trust her. We should send her back to wherever she came from."

"I'm sure there must be a good reason," Miranda says.

"And she's clearly terrified, too," Alfred adds.

"Every second we stay with you, we're in danger," Mrs. Rodan says. "We can't risk it. I'm sorry."

See how your compassion is repaid? Dar hisses. *They have no appreciation for what you did for them.*

Alarm floods my veins, and I let out a small gasp. They all turn to stare at me. I'd like nothing more than to disappear into the cave floor.

"Cary, Doyle, we're leaving now before it's too late," Mr. Rodan says.

Lucas's parents don't make any move to stop them, and they set off without another word. Cary shoots daggers at me with her eyes as she leaves the cave, but Doyle regards me curiously. When they're gone, Lucas and his parents focus their full attention on me.

"Emmeline, are you all right?" Lucas crouches down next to me, worry creasing his face.

I scramble to my feet, casting an anxious look between them. "I believe so," I say.

I am greeted with silence, and a knot forms in my stomach. Alfred speaks first, shoving his glasses back up the bridge of his nose. "Emmeline, why didn't you warn us that the soldiers searching for you also worked for Lady Aisling the first time they came for you?" He crosses his arms over his chest. "You put Lucas and Doyle in grave danger, not to mention yourself."

The accusation hits me like a bucket of cold water. And I can say nothing to deny it either.

My mouth flops open helplessly.

"How did you know those soldiers worked for Lady Aisling?" Miranda asks with a pained look on her face. "We suspected, but you knew who they were well enough to warn us last night that Lady Aisling had come."

Don't do it, Emmeline, don't tell them anything. Deny it! Dar insists, but I find that I cannot. I'm weary of keeping things from these people I've grown to care for. Lying to them now would be an even worse betrayal.

I hang my head. "I'm sorry," I begin. "Please don't send me home. You don't understand, they'll take everything from me."

"Why didn't you tell us the truth earlier? We could have taken precautions. We could have been on our way long before last night." Miranda shakes her head and turns away.

"What do you have to say for yourself?" Alfred says.

Please don't tell, Dar whispers so fearfully that it nearly brings tears to my eyes. If they knew everything I've done to help Dar—stealing things, sneaking out at night—they'd be even more furious.

"One of Lady Aisling's nobles visited my family's estate last week. His name is Tate," I say, choosing my words carefully. "He discovered my talent and my parents' disgust for it when I was caught eavesdropping on him. He told my parents he could cure me, and they were going to send me away. I had no choice but to run. I couldn't stand the thought of losing my talent."

Lucas reaches out and places a hand on my arm. His face is grim, something I've never seen on him before.

Alfred frowns. "Why didn't you tell us this? What else are you hiding?"

Heat flashes up and down my body. I can't tell them the rest without explaining Dar. And that just won't do.

"I've never left home before. I was terrified and didn't know who to trust. Please don't leave me alone," is all I can safely say.

Lucas sits down next to me while Miranda and Alfred

exchange a resigned look and walk to the other side of the cave. They talk in low voices but we can still hear them.

"Our home has been destroyed. Usually we have a new one ready to go before we move, but not this time," Alfred says.

"All our possessions are destroyed too," Miranda says. "We've remained under the radar only because Lady Aisling doesn't know about Lucas. But she knows about Emmeline, that much is clear, and she will never stop hunting her until she finds her. We've seen it before."

My skin grows cold, and even Dar's fierce hug cannot warm me. All I can see is the memory of Simone's pale, haunted face.

"It isn't your fault." Lucas glares at his parents' backs. "You couldn't possibly have known what they would do, how far they would go."

His words pierce my heart and I try to speak. "I—"

"They're going to send you home, I know it."

My breath halts in my lungs and I gape at Lucas. His face is deadly serious.

"They're going to do it to protect me. That's always the deciding factor in every decision they make."

Dar screams in my ears. *Go! Run before they try anything. They can't be trusted!*

I swallow hard, trying to shut her out. "I would be very sad to leave you, if they do. At home, my only friends are shadows. It's been nice getting to know you and your family." Heat burns behind my eyes.

"I won't let them do it," Lucas says grabbing my hand. "Come on, Emmeline. We need to go before they make up their minds." He tugs me out of the cave toward the woods, but not before Miranda notices.

"Lucas! Wait!" she cries.

"We're not abandoning my friend!" he yells back. Tears burn my eyes. But I don't stop him. The terrible, dark part of me can't bear to.

Don't say a word, Dar warns. *Not until we've done the ritual. Then you can tell him everything. Please, keep me safe just a little longer.*

I do as my shadow insists and stay silent, though not for the reasons she thinks. Dar knew who those soldiers were and what they meant. She knows more about Lady Aisling than she has let on. And yet she tried to convince me to leave Lucas and his friends behind to her mercy. I can't trust Dar anymore. Maybe it will change when she's made flesh again, but not like this.

But Lucas, with his light that slips into every word and deed, I can.

We dodge through the forest while Lucas's parents shout his name behind us. I feel sicker with every step, but his are determined, carrying us farther and farther away.

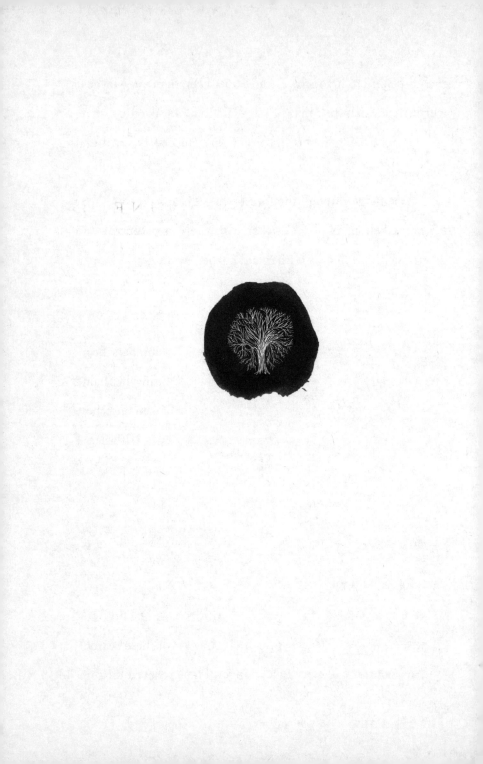

CHAPTER TWENTY-ONE

Night fell hours ago, and now Lucas slumbers near the fire, the light from the flames teasing his hair. I'd be sleeping too if Dar hadn't woken me, her cool, smoky fingers insistent that we get up. Lucas fell asleep with his hand in mine, and I have not yet risen, not wanting to let go.

We have one more task to complete before we can perform the ritual, Dar says. *Then, no more secrets, no more lies. There will be no need.* A gap forms in the shape of a smile.

Until recently, I've been thrilled by the idea of Dar becoming flesh and blood like me. But the weight of all these secrets is too heavy for me to carry much longer. I'll be relieved for this to be over and done. She has become so jealous and strange. Last night, she knew the guards were near, but her only priority was stealing Miranda's supplies that we needed. She didn't even want me to save my other friends.

She would have been perfectly happy for them to be captured by Lady Aisling. And I fear Lucas and Miranda's nightmares were not nightmares at all; that Dar did something to them like she did to Lord Tate.

With one wistful gaze back at Lucas, I pluck a few shadows to cloak me and we head into the woods.

"Where do we go tonight?" I whisper to Dar, careful to be quiet just in case the soldiers are still about. A quick burst of guilt hits me that I've left Lucas alone, but there is no help for it now.

We only have to collect water blessed by the full blood moon. We passed a pond on our flight from Lucas's family.

Her words trouble me. Lucas's parents are good and kind and Dar's tone suggests a certain sort of glee at being free of them. If anything, I miss them already.

We trudge through the woods, exhaustion making me sway. I've used a lot of magic in the past few days, and had so little sleep that it seems to be taking a larger toll than I expected. I've always used my magic daily before, but perhaps the lack of sleep is the culprit.

Don't worry, Dar says, *it isn't far. This will soon be over.*

She wraps her cool arms around me, and I lean into the gesture. When she is flesh again, I shall hug her for real.

The moon is full and bright over our heads and turns a deep crimson the higher it rises, tainting the shadows red. So this is what Dar meant by a blood moon. There is something unsettling about it, but I swallow my uneasiness and push forward. Soon I see a flash of silver between the trees. Relieved, I begin to run, or try to with halting steps. The small bottle Dar insisted we borrow from Miranda's cabinets is in my pocket. All I need to do is fill it and then go back to Lucas and let sleep take me away from this regret.

When the woods break, my shadows converge on me. I drop to my knees beside the pond. My face reflects in the water and I realize with a start how much I've changed. The girl who gazes back is not the same one who left her parents' home. That girl was soft and coddled.

The new girl has dirt smudged on her nose, and cuts from

branches dot her arms and cheeks. And her hollow eyes sink into her face like something has been slowly draining the life from her.

Dar hovers over my shoulder, but she has no reflection in the still waters. *It is only the lack of sleep. Soon you will be as robust as ever.*

Is it? Or has something caused this, just like I fear Dar may have caused Lucas and Miranda's nightmares? I shiver, then dip the small bottle in the cool water, disturbing the girl in the reflection. I didn't like the way she gazed back at me. Something about her was haunted and hunted.

I stopper the bottle and slip it into my pocket. A hoard of shadows wriggles in the trees. My magic must be leaking from me in my exhaustion, calling them near when I don't have a need. But they are sweet shadows desiring a little attention. I brush through them, letting my fingers trail over their edges in greeting, silently sending them back where they belong and bidding them goodnight.

The trek back to our little makeshift camp is a blur. My mind floats from worry to worry, and I begin to babble on to Dar about this and that as I weave through the trees.

"Do you think Lucas will forgive me?" I ask her.

If he has any sense he will, she says.

I stumble into the clearing where we camped and come face to face with a very awake and stunned Lucas. He holds my flour sack, and the rose and mortar and pestle I took from his mother are on the ground beside it. All the muscles in my chest clench, tearing my breath from my lungs.

He finds the words to speak first. "Who were you talking to just now?"

A scream claws at my throat. This isn't how I wanted him to find out.

Don't tell him, Emmeline, don't—

"But I have to, Dar," I admonish my shadow, making Lucas flinch. I have no other way to explain the contents of my bag. Perhaps if I can make him see it is in pursuit of a worthy cause he will forgive me. Maybe he'll even help me.

"What—who—what are you doing with all these things?" Lucas holds up the rotting apple then drops it back into the sack in disgust.

I step closer, but Dar slips away and sulks near the tree line. "You know what I can do with shadows, Lucas. I'm a shadow weaver. But there is something else about me that I haven't told you. I was afraid. Other people have… They've feared and ridiculed me for it." My gaze lingers on the fire pit, which is beginning to sputter out.

Lucas sets the sack aside. "Why?"

I sit next to him carefully, like he's some kind of timid animal I might frighten away. "My shadow."

"Emmeline, you're not making sense. What are you doing with all these weird things in your bag?"

I twist the shadows cast by my fingers into knots. "My own shadow is alive. She talks to me. And I can talk to her. She has been my best friend my whole life. Even when my parents tried to pretend I didn't exist she was there for me."

Lucas recoils. "How can that—how can that be?"

"Dar," I say. "Come here."

I don't wish to, she says petulantly.

I sigh. "Dar, come here. Now."

But she slides farther away until only a thin string connects us. I could pull her back, force her to come to me, but what would that prove? I can't make her talk to Lucas.

"I'm the only who can hear her. It has something to do

with my shadow magic. She's a lost soul now, but she was human once."

Lucas's eyes widen. "What happened?"

"Lady Aisling." I scowl.

His face pales. "You knew about Lady Aisling and what she could do all along?"

My heart sinks.

I told you not to tell him, Dar says, drifting back to my feet.

"I couldn't tell you. Dar was one of Lady Aisling's first victims. She became a lost soul as a result. But she found me the night I was born, drawn to my magic. What I told your parents was the truth—the Lady's ambassador, Lord Tate, tried to get my parents to send me away with him. He was going to take away my shadow magic. Dar said she could help. I was desperate. She didn't mean for it to happen, but Tate ended up in a coma. They sent for soldiers from Zinnia, and that's when we ran away."

Lucas skitters back, his expression hardening as the words I've wished to tell him for too long tumble from my lips.

"But that doesn't explain any of this." He waves his hand over my flour sack. My stomach twists.

"I promised Dar that I would help her become flesh and blood again. I've been collecting these things because I need them to perform a ritual that will restore her." I scoot closer and reach for his hand, but he yanks it back. "Please understand, Dar is the only friend I've had since I was a baby. I can't bear the thought of her being trapped as a shadow when she used to be human. I need to make it right. And when she's whole again, she can fix what happened with Lady Aisling's ambassador. She can put everything right, and then I can go home again."

A lump in my throat swells, and I choke on the tears that threaten. Out here, facing Lucas, I miss home more than I ever have. I wish all of this had never happened.

Lucas's face falls. "Weren't *we* friends?" He scrambles to his feet. "Why didn't you ask for help? You took my mother's mortar and pestle. Those are family heirlooms. She needs them to make tonics and poultices to sell at the market. I'm sure if you'd just asked to borrow them she would have lent them to you happily." He scoffs. "But instead, you hid things from us. We took you in. You lied about knowing who Lady Aisling is."

"It was only because of Dar. You didn't hear how she

pleaded with me to keep her a secret. I couldn't betray my lifelong friend." I get to my feet, desperation settling into my limbs.

Lucas takes another step away. "No, but it was fine for you to betray *us*. Don't you understand? They could have caught me! Or Doyle. Lady Aisling might have stolen my magic by now." He shudders. "The Rodans were right. This is your fault. All of it. I don't know if that shadow of yours is real or not, but if she is then it's her fault too. You deserve each other."

He snatches his knapsack from the ground and flees into the woods.

"No, Lucas, wait! I didn't mean it like that!" I start after him, but Dar stops me.

Let him be. We are better off without him. He won't trust you again after finding his mother's things in your possession.

My stomach drops into my feet, and I sink back onto one of the logs near the dying fire. Understanding burns through my chest. That must be the real reason Dar wanted me to take those things of Miranda's; if I was caught, it would—and did—drive a wedge between me and my new friends.

Lucas is right. This *is* my fault. I've known it, felt it all along, but somehow managed to hold the brunt of it at bay. He and his family treated me so kindly that I thought for a moment that maybe I deserved it. Maybe I wasn't too awful.

I was wrong.

Wrapping my arms around my knees, I watch the fire until the coals are black and all the light and warmth I've craved for so long has vanished.

CHAPTER TWENTY-TWO

hey never deserved your trust, Dar says in my ears. *I would never desert you, no matter what.* She curls around my shoulders as I race through the trees, heedless of the direction. When the fire finally died, my only thought was to get away. But there is no outrunning the burning in my eyes and the disgust billowing in my gut.

I thought of all of them, Lucas was the one I could trust to understand me. To have some empathy for my predicament. But I'll never forget the awful, crushed expression on his face when he realized what I've done.

When did I become a liar and a thief? I did it all for a good cause. Or at least I thought I did. I just want to set things right, back the way they used to be before my world exploded.

A horse braying nearby halts my tracks. I pull my shadows close as quickly as possible, but not fast enough.

"There she is!" cries one of the soldiers. A flash of ghostly white—Simone—peeks out from the group of guards, sending a chill straight down to my marrow.

I flee, gathering more shadows with each step as fear coils inside my chest, ready to spring and strangle me. I dodge and weave, circling back over my tracks repeatedly to throw off any dogs they might have with them.

We are so close to making Dar flesh again. I can't risk being caught now. I don't know how long we run, but finally we are far enough away that I can't hear the hoofbeats any longer, and my breath rasps through my lungs.

Dar's cool fingers weave through my hair as we hide from the pursuing guards between the shadows in the woods. If they still have Simone with them, we will not remain hidden for long.

We must do something.

Trust me, Dar whispers. *When everyone else fails you, I am still here. Always.*

"I do trust you," I whisper back. How can I not? I've been left with no one else.

I was a fool. I should have told Lucas and his family about Dar from the moment I chose to confide in them. But I was scared they'd fear me.

If they loved you, they would have forgiven you. They'd never have abandoned you. I always forgive you. You know that.

I dodge between shadows, desperate to keep moving, even while I remain hidden.

"What do you think we should do now, Dar? I'm terrified of being taken by those soldiers." I've been holding that dread inside for days, letting it stew and coil until it has become a fearsome thing.

There is only one thing we can do: perform the ritual.

My breath stops. Of course, the ritual.

The full blood moon is out, and you have all the ingredients in your bag. We must perform the ritual immediately. Then I can protect you from the guards.

A sudden desperation seizes my legs, and I begin to run again, headlong through the woods, hoping to put as much distance between me and the pursuing soldiers as I possibly can. Just to give myself enough time to perform the ritual—and whatever that may entail—so Dar can protect us. She'll know what to do.

She had shape shifting magic when she was human. Perhaps that will come back with her true form. I may not trust her motives, but I have no reason to doubt that when she says she can protect us, she means it.

I stop when I reach a small grove deep in the forest, then I empty the contents of the flour sack in the middle of the grass. The rose and the now rotten apple, the witch hazel and the flask of water, Miranda's mortar and pestle, and of course the three candles I stole from the temple of the Cerelia Comet.

"What must I do to perform the ritual?" Despite our situation, my blood fizzes with excitement. Tonight my best friend will be real again. My whole life, I have secretly harbored this wish, and now it will come true. We can put all these terrible lies behind us at last. Maybe if I can introduce Lucas and his family to Dar when she's flesh and blood, they will understand and forgive me.

My shadow transforms into a slow grin, a half-moon widening over the grass. *Put the apple, the witch hazel, and the water into the mortar and grind it up into a paste.*

I do as she instructs, wrinkling my nose at the sickly sweet smell of the rotting apple.

"What do I do with this?" I ask, picking up the rose. "Ouch!" I accidentally prick my thumb on one of the thorns. A large bead of blood drops into the bowl. "Oh, no, Dar, did I just ruin—"

Perfect, she says. *You did just what you were supposed to do. Now take three of the petals and crush them up in the bowl too.*

"Lucas's mother really loved her rose garden," I murmur, the vision of it turning to ash searing into the back of my brain.

Well, it's gone now, isn't it? Dar says.

Surprised by the venom in her voice, tears well in my eyes. Several drop into the bowl. "Dar, why—"

Tears of regret are the second to last ingredient.

Something hot and sticky and tight forms over my chest.

"What is the last ingredient?"

A hair from your head.

"And that's it?"

Simply mix it all up and light the candles.

"But why must a shadow weaver do it then?"

After the mixture is complete and the candles lit, you must spread the paste over my shadow form. No one else but you can touch me. Then cocoon me in shadows.

I give my shadow's arm a squeeze and an encouraging smile that I don't feel at all, then pluck a hair from my head. The pain only lasts for a second, but the prick in my finger still throbs from where the thorn dug in.

I ignore it, my whole focus on the mixture and listening for sounds of pursuit coming from the woods. I know the soldiers are hunting me. It is only a matter of time until they find me.

I light the candles with some matches I took, and then begin to cover Dar's entire form with the mess of a paste. I pray I did it right.

What happens if I messed it up? Put the ingredients together in the wrong order? What if we waited too long between collecting ingredients or not long enough?

What will Dar look like when she's fully human again?

A thousand questions chase each other through my mind. But none of them will be answered until the ritual is complete.

By the time I feel the ground beneath my knees throbbing with hoofbeats, I am almost done and my shadow is covered in the brown, goopy mess. I dab the last bit of the paste on the edge of Dar's form and sit back to examine my work. Now instead of a shadow she looks like a creature fashioned from a strange smelling mud.

Now, surround me with bands of your shadows.

I pull the shadows from the nearest trees, wrapping them around Dar's form like bandages until she's covered head to toe.

Dar laughs with glee in my head and begins to murmur.

Witch hazel, harvested in darkness,

Stolen fruit, rotten to the core…

Dar's form begins to bubble through the bands of shadows. Up from the mud a face takes shape, like a human stuck deep in the field finally breaking free. I gasp and scramble to my feet.

Water, blessed by the full blood moon,

Roses, pinched from a garden,

Misbegotten candles, tears of regret, blood of a thief, and hair from a liar's head,

Come together under the full moon…

"…and make me whole!"

Chills run up and down my arms as I hear her voice out loud for the first time in the last line of the incantation. More of her shape rises from the ground, plumping and rounding and expanding, absorbing the shadows I wrapped around her into her new form. She almost looks like a maiden in a fairy tale, slumbering away for centuries under the earth.

Or she would if it wasn't for her murmuring lips. She repeats the words over and over, each refrain burning into my ears.

This must be some dark magic she has had me do. My hands begin to shake, and without thinking I clutch the nearest shadows for comfort. Dar's form moved with me before, but this time she remains stuck to the ground, her shape coalescing more with every second that passes.

When she finally stops changing shapes and is just a girl coated in mud lying on the ground, she ceases her murmuring. Her fingers twitch, and I jump back a step. Then her eyes flare open, and she grins.

It reminds me of an animal baring its teeth, not the happy smile I'd hoped to see.

She wiggles her toes, then bends her arms and begins laughing. It isn't the laugh I've heard in my head all these years. It is colder, thinner, no weight behind it.

No mirth in it at all.

Then she uses her arms and legs to crawl up to her feet.

There's something animalistic in the way she moves, like she is a hungry hunter on the prowl. I swallow hard. That isn't true. She is a girl, just like me.

Dar stands before me, covered in mud, gobs of the stinking mixture falling off her, revealing bits of skin and pieces of an old-fashioned dress. It may have once been white, but now it is gray and brown and beyond recovery. She is a little taller than me, and her hair seems to be brown, but that could also be the effect of the mud. Her eyes are flat, straight black with no whites at all. As though that was the one part of her that could not throw off the shadow form entirely.

"Thank you, Emmeline," Dar says, and it is the strangest thing to hear her voice, here, in the open where anyone passing by could hear her speak too. "You have done very well, indeed."

I blink at her, uncertain what to do. Her body vibrates with an energy I never imagined she possessed.

Finally, I find my words again. "Are you all right?"

She laughs, then shakes her hair and body, and much of the mixture flies off in every direction. I wipe a speck of the gross stuff from my dress.

"Now, sweet Emmeline," Dar says, flashing me a feral grin. She begins to change before my eyes, slowly becoming less girl-like and more...something else. "I am ready to take my revenge."

CHAPTER TWENTY-THREE

Revenge?" Alarm fills me with a fever pitch. "What do you mean?"

The awful figure who was once my friend approaches, ballooning in size before my eyes.

"What—what are you?" I choke out.

Dar laughs with a horrible cackle. "I am anything I choose to be."

I take a step back, unsure whether anything—even my shadows—can offer protection now. "What do you want from me?"

She raises an eyebrow. "From you? Emmeline, you've already given me what I need." She grins. "I have everything I require for my vengeance."

"On who?"

She paces the grove in a circle around me. "My sister, Lady Aisling."

Terror holds me in its grip, rendering me unable to move in the face of this creature I've set loose. What happened to the girl I thought I was bringing back to life? Where has my best friend gone?

"Oh, yes, I've known all along what she is. What she has done. Those children Lucas's parents told you about? She took them after me. She stole them to use, to take their magic. Just like she stole mine."

Sickly understanding sinks in. "You lied." It is hard to breathe, and I can barely get the words out. "What you told me about how you died. Was any of it true?"

She shrugs. "Of sorts. I discovered I could change shapes at an early age. Aisling was always jealous of me. We were born on the same day. She didn't figure out what her magic was until she was older. She's a magic eater. She can call the talents of other people out and use it as her own. She devoured mine first, but she didn't realize how tied it was to my very being. She took everything I was in the process, every shred of goodness and light in me, and left my soul floating in darkness."

Dar kicks a wayward branch so hard it strikes a nearby tree and splinters. I flinch. "But from those shadows I saw what she became. With every talent she stole, she grew more powerful, more ravenous. The second talent she took was from a child who could make plants grow. Somehow, she managed to combine that with her siphoning magic and…"

Dar breaks off, and even the shadows flee from her and the terrible expression on her face.

"She what?" I whisper.

"She is greedy. And wants a steady stream of power. She transforms talented children into flowers, planting them in her Garden of Souls. They remain alive, ever blooming, and she can pluck some of their power away when she chooses. But sometimes the process doesn't work, and it obliterates their minds instead. Those become shells and pawns, like that little girl Simone."

Horror claws up my throat, but I find I cannot scream. Cannot say a word.

"She keeps them, all her pretty little children, in her

renowned garden that all the nobles fawn over." Dar scoffs. "They have no idea what the flowers really are. She has been living off their magic for one hundred years. Seeking out talented children, scouring the countryside, and harvesting any new ones as they are born. Your parents hated your magic and kept you secret as much as possible." She stops her pacing, and I can't quite tell whether she's grinning or baring her teeth at me. "It was a happy circumstance for me when I found you. Finally, someone who could see me. Who could touch me after so many years in solitude. I knew you'd be the one to make me flesh again."

Her eyes glitter with a light I've never seen before, and it stings me to the core. She has been lying to me since the second I met her.

"You were using me, all along. All those years?" Tears slide down my cheeks and I brush them away.

She never loved me at all, not like I loved her.

I wrap my arms around my stomach, trying to hold in the sudden onslaught of suffocating hurt.

A terrible grin swims over Dar's face. "Oh yes. You have no idea how useful you were. My sister left me hollow, a lost soul clinging to this world fueled only by hate. I needed more negative emotions—ephemeral, delicious things—to keep me alive. You, so naive, so trusting, so desperate for kinship, made it easy." She tilts her head at me, like an animal on the hunt. "Every lie you told, every trick and game we played, the hate your parents grew to feel for you, the fear of the servants—all of these things sustained me, emboldened me these last few years in a way nothing else had before."

In a brutal torrent, several mysterious events connect. Rose's fatal accident, Tate's coma, even Lucas's nightmares and Miranda's headaches—any time someone got close to me or threatened to separate us, something bad happened to them. Every single time.

My legs fail me, and I sink to the ground in the middle of the grove. My parents. They feared me, but they pushed me away because of the things Dar had convinced me to do. And the things she did when I wasn't looking. Every game and trick was a wedge between us until the gulf became too wide to bridge.

Would my parents have loved me, been proud of me, if not for Dar whispering deceit in my ears?

Dar glides closer. "Don't cry, Emmeline. We can be together now. We can take our revenge on Lady Aisling together."

I shake my head, wishing I could shake her words out of my ears. "All I wanted to do was cure Tate and return home. Was that a lie too?"

Dar laughs. "Why would I want to cure one of my sister's minions? Tate is as bad as she is. Mark my words—if she gets her claws into you or your little friend Lucas, you'll live to regret it. You'll live a very long time, without hope, without the ability to move or scream. It will be a living hell as her plaything."

I straighten up, playing at the courage I wish I felt. "That isn't going to happen. Lucas and his family are off to hide again, and now I know to hide too. I won't let her take me. I can escape into the shadows. I'm safe."

Dar stares at me for a long moment, frighteningly still. "Foolish child. While Lady Aisling lives, no one with a talent is safe."

Fierce resolve fills me. "I won't join you in revenge. For all I know this is just another trick. I have hurt enough people at your behest. Never again."

"Then you will regret it." She pauses, her ears perking and

transforming for a moment into ones that resemble a wolf. I gasp. She wasn't lying about being a shape shifter at least.

Then she smiles wickedly. "They're here."

Before I can respond, she begins to shift into something new, something enormous.

Something I actually recognize.

Her favorite shape when we played games and startled unsuspecting servants, the same one we used on Kendra when she twisted her ankle: a gigantic, beastly monster. Her body expands, her face twists into a snout, and her hair becomes giant horns. Her arms elongate, muscles twining around them, ending in wicked, sharp talons. Her feet are clawed paws.

I gape.

When I hear what spurred this change—the approaching soldiers—she grins at me, her mouth now filled with row upon row of razor sharp teeth.

"No," I whisper. My voice transforms into a scream. "No!" She just laughs, but in her new form it sounds more like a howl.

The soldiers appear, positioning their horses to surround us. Simone is nowhere in sight this time. They must have split up to cover more ground. The animals rear and whinny at Dar's fearsome new appearance.

"A shifter?" says one, and I recognize him as Alden, Tate's nephew. "Haven't seen of one of those in a long time. Simone was right. My Lady will be very pleased to see you."

Dar growls. A soldier launches a net in her direction, but one flick of her claws slices it in half. I hold my breath.

"Leave them alone," I say, but I'm petrified that they will take me too. I don't see this ending well for any of us.

"Never," she barks. "Remember, Emmeline? I promised to protect you." Without warning she dives into them, sweeping the nearest off their horses. The animals flee, afraid they'll be next, no doubt. She throws her head back and howls, her horns brushing against the upper limbs of the trees, then plunges back into the fray.

She is a mass of fur and claws and speed. I can barely keep my eyes on her.

Then someone grabs me from behind, throwing a net around me like I'm some kind of animal. "No! Help!" I twist around to see one of the soldiers with a frantic expression on his face.

"I've got her, sir! I—"

Dar yanks him off the ground and tosses him into the forest. I am so stunned by his sudden disappearance that I don't even flinch when Dar slices the netting off me.

"Run, Emmeline." Her breath, hot and stale, hits me in the face.

My heart flails in my chest, every beat fanning the flames of panic. Every nerve says to bolt, but I can't let Dar hurt anyone else.

I need help.

I shudder, my stomach turning at the sight of Dar and the soldiers fighting. Then I finally do as Dar instructed: I run.

I run from soldiers who'd hand me over to Lady Aisling, and I run from the monster who was my whole world.

But most of all, I flee from the mess I've made.

CHAPTER TWENTY-FOUR

Right now, the need to find Lucas and his family reverberates through every fiber of my body. He was right. His parents and friends were right.

And I was so, so wrong.

I'll need his help to get Dar under control. I set her free, and it's my responsibility to ensure she doesn't hurt anyone else ever again.

I only hope that Dar is wrong and that my new friends will forgive me.

I tear through the forest, running in the direction I last saw Lucas leaving. I have to find him, warn him and his family, just in case Dar decides I've betrayed her and blames them.

The moon lights my path in the early morning hours. Shadows swirl around me in greeting, dodging through my hair and cloaking me as securely as I could wish. My magic seems to obey my thoughts unconsciously now.

I pause in a clearing to get my bearings, and a sudden shocking revelation nearly brings me to my knees: I no longer cast a shadow.

My shadow, my companion for my whole life, is utterly gone. It must have become so inextricably linked to Dar that it transformed as part of her during the ritual. A tiny part of myself that will always be with her. Maybe, just maybe, it will lend her a small piece of my conscience too.

For the first time in my life I am alone. Really, truly alone. No constant presence at my side, no voice echoing in my head. This feeling—solitude—is a strange and lonely thing that hollows out my insides.

But I don't have the luxury of time to think on this now. I regain my composure, then begin to craft a hound from the shadows that follow me. Once it is wagging its tail on the forest floor in front of me, I give it the scent of Lucas and his family, still lingering on my clothes, and set it running through the woods to track them.

It bounds away, and I chase after, my steps swift and fueled by a burgeoning sense of terror. The shadow hound leads me on a circuitous route through the woods, sometimes looping back on itself, then pausing to catch the scent again before bounding away in a new direction. I do not know how long or how far we run, but when the shadow hound finally stops not far from an outcropping of rocks, I pause to catch my breath. My heart pulses in my ears, blood and adrenaline racing through my veins. The single spot on my forefinger that was pricked by the rose throbs too, a pinching reminder of what I've done.

I dismiss the shadow hound, letting the shadows return to cloak me instead. I creep toward the rocks, doing my best to steady my breath.

Something white flashes between the rocks and I halt in my tracks.

It happens again and this time I see it more clearly. It is a girl, ghostly and pale, with hair like a frizzy sort of shroud.

Simone.

I duck behind the nearest tree, shivering. I don't understand how, but whatever Lady Aisling did to that girl makes it possible for her to see through my shadows. If she is near, then the rest of the soldiers must be too. This could be their encampment.

My heart drops into my boots.

And if the shadow hound led me here, then Lucas and his family are here as well.

They've been caught.

My eyes burn with frustration and unshed tears. I have to fix this. I must free them. I'll just need to get past Simone to do it.

I peer out from the tree to see Simone's flashes of dull white every few minutes as she winds between the rocks. From where I stand, I see no sign of soldiers or Lucas and his family. I dash from tree to tree until I circle farther around the outcropping. A soldier or two is hidden in the woods on guard duty, but unlike Simone, they can't see through my shadows. Between those and the darkness of the night, I'm protected from discovery.

When I reach the opposite side of the rock formation, I finally see them. The soldiers have set up camp in the perfect spot so that the rocks in the woods conceal them from anyone passing by. Like me.

At the center of the camp, three figures are huddled around a tree trunk, tied together with rope. Cold foreboding sweeps over my body. It's them, Lucas and his parents. I had hoped I might be wrong.

I ball my hands into fists at my sides, shadows swirling around my wrists, ready to heed my bidding.

An idea sparks inside my brain. If I can get enough shadows together, then—

"I know you, I know you," says a singsong voice in my ear. I gasp, spinning around and scrambling backward. Simone, her dull white frock swaying in the nighttime breeze, stands behind me with a wild grin over her face.

She frowns. "You're missing something," she whispers, and tilts her head to the side. She draws in a deep breath like she's getting ready to yell. I cannot allow that to happen. It would bring the soldiers running, and disrupt my plan before I've even started.

With hardly a second thought, the shadows around my wrists transform into tacky material and I fling them at her.

One shadow flattens over her mouth, holding in her scream. Her eyes go wide and she scrabbles at the shadow holding her voice inside. Then the others wrap around her wrists, drawing her back and pinning her to the nearest tree.

She struggles but can't break free of them. Then she stops struggling and sighs. The shadow still allows her to breathe but doesn't release its grip on her mouth.

There is more curious light in her eyes right now than I ever saw when she was traipsing around my parents' house. I take a step closer. I can't help wondering what talent she once had that made Lady Aisling desperate to steal it and landed her in such a state. The girl feels as odd and empty to me as ever, but now I view her with more pity than I did before.

"What did she do to you?" I say, knowing she can't answer. Simone stares blankly at me. "Do you help them willingly? Or are you as much a captive as the ones she keeps in her garden?"

Simone's eyes flash at that question and she goes very still. She doesn't even blink, almost like she is trying to send me a message.

If I know you, then she knows you, a small grim voice echoes in my head, startling me. Followed quickly by an odd pang of loss. I'll never hear Dar's voice in my head like that again.

"Was that your talent? Getting in people's heads?"

Simone slowly nods, her eyes never leaving mine.

"Then how did you—" I frown. "You could sense my mind, that's how you did it, isn't it? That's how you could see through my shadows. You could sense my mind...and Dar's."

The girl's eyes brighten and she nods again.

"Do you want to be free of her? The Lady? If you help me, maybe I can help you."

This time Simone's eyes go wide and sorrowful.

My mind is not my own. Do not trust me. She looks as if she has swallowed poison, and I shudder. How awful is it to not be in control of one's own mind?

"Is it painful to use your magic then, to communicate mind to mind?"

She nods.

An awful thought tears through me, halting my breath. "Does she know we're talking?"

Tears pinch at the corners of Simone's eyes. She nods again.

Suddenly her eyes go wide, then blank. Her gaze has always been unsettling but this time it's different.

And so is the voice resonating in my head.

Where is my sister?

The hair raises on the back of my neck.

What did you do with her, girl? the voice says more forcefully. *Give her to me, and I will let your friends go.*

I step backward, my hands quivering at my side, and I yank more shadows to me as if that could hide me from discovery. After all I've learned, I have no doubt Lady Aisling is controlling Simone.

And she wants Dar.

Simone's first words to us—*I know you*—hit me with the full force of their true meaning. Lady Aisling was using her as a puppet all along. Somehow, she recognized Dar even though she was only a shadow.

And she has been pursuing us ever since.

Carefully, I duck behind a tree. The voice in my head laughs. *That boy, the light singer, will make a fine addition to my Garden.* The last word ends in a snarl. *Maybe a sunflower.*

I can hear Simone's body struggling against the bonds tying her to the tree. Lady Aisling must be in full control now; the poor girl is nothing more than a puppet. I move as quickly as I can, traveling behind the tree Simone is stuck to so that she (and Lady Aisling) can't tell for certain which direction I've gone. I wish I could help the girl, but I'm not sure how. By her own admission, I can't trust her.

When I find the outcropping where I first spotted Simone, I move closer to the camp, feeling a little safer knowing that she is tied up, and I am out of her line of sight. I can no longer hear Lady Aisling or Simone's voice in my head, so her power must be limited to a range. Which is a relief because that will also make it difficult for them to warn the guards.

From my new vantage point, I can see more of the camp. Only a few guards remain awake, gathered around a fire in the center. The rest must sleep in the tents scattered throughout the rocks or are fighting Dar back in the glade. Lucas and his family are tied up a short ways behind the soldiers on watch.

I keep my shadows close at hand so I can deploy my plan. Fully encased in them, I creep into the camp with bated breath and tingling skin.

Every step is a nightmare. This is not the first time I have snuck past these guards, but it is the first time I've done it without Dar to warn me, guard me, and guide me. Despite the newfound knowledge that she has been using me all these years,

I can't help feeling as though I've lost one of my limbs. Some necessary piece of me is missing.

And I'll never get it back.

But I keep moving anyway. I must do this by myself, and I'll need to get used to it fast.

I am halfway across the camp when raucous laughter rings out from the group of soldiers near the fire. I freeze, panic sliding over my skin like oil. One of them heads toward a nearby tent. He passes so close that I don't dare move, don't dare breathe. If he walks into me, I'm caught.

He passes within inches of where I stand without giving me a second look. When he enters the tent and the flap closes behind him, I finally let out my breath, feeling rather lightheaded.

I press on, emboldened by my success, but still weak in the knees from fear. Now that I know what Lady Aisling does, what would really happen, much more is at stake than my talent of shadow weaving. I can't be as naive as I was the first time I snuck away from my parents' estate.

Up ahead, Lucas dozes off by the tree like he's trying to keep watch and it isn't quite working. His parents appear to be sleeping. A gag is wrapped around his mouth, probably to prevent him from using his lightcraft. Venom tears through me—I hate the fact that Lady Aisling knows about him, after all his parents have done to keep him safe. All I can hope is that they don't spurn me now. I'll do anything I can to keep them from Lady Aisling's grasp.

I am only a foot away when I stop. Lucas hasn't seen me yet, and I can't let my shadows down for a second for fear the guards might glimpse me too. But there is another way to show him I'm here.

Inside my cloak of shadows, I pull a couple together, twisting and twining them into a shape Lucas will recognize. Then I set the shadow on the ground and send it bounding over to my friend.

The shadow puppy dances over, pawing at Lucas's legs. I've made it tangible enough for him to feel it. His eyes widen, and he twists his head. Almost as soon as he starts, he thinks better of it and stops. No need to let the guards in on my rescue attempt. At least not yet.

But now his eyes are alight with hope.

The shadows are still tinged with the red of the blood moon high overhead. I craft three more shadows, plucking more material from the deepening dark of the night. Within minutes, they are ready to release. I set one loose, and it floats toward Lucas and his parents. Lucas watches with wonder as it settles onto his chest, then expands to cover his full shape, becoming a shadow doppelganger, a nearly identical copy of his own form. Shading even gives the appearance of features at a glance.

Then I kneel down next to him and hurry to loosen his bonds. I have no weapons, nothing to fight with except my shadows. But luckily I'm not too shabby with knots and his come undone quickly. He rubs his wrists and smiles, understanding that it isn't safe to talk. I reach out a hand and pull him into my shadow cloak, widening it to cover both of us completely. The shadow doppelganger I crafted remains at the base of the tree, and even has shadow ropes holding it down.

Lucas wakes up his parents, while I set their own shadow doppelgangers loose, then we free them from their bonds too.

In minutes, we are all under cloaking shadows, tiptoeing back across the camp. But as we pass the tent where the guard disappeared earlier, the flap flies open and he steps out, nearly colliding with Alfred, hidden under the shadows.

The guard has a strange expression on his face. With a

sinking heart I follow his gaze: he's squinting at the tree where Lucas and his family were imprisoned minutes earlier.

We move faster as the guard walks over, then lets up a shout. "Hey! Where did they go?!" The shadows that had taken their forms dissolve into smoke, and we stop completely. All we need is a broken branch snapping under our feet to give us away. I must do something else to distract the guards.

Breathless, Lucas and his parents exchange looks of terror under the shadow cloak, while I take more shadow material from the forest to weave. These too I craft into something I haven't done much of before until tonight—human forms. I had Dar; what need did I have of other human-like shadows that didn't talk? But tonight I hope they will serve me well.

I mirror the forms of the guards using the tall trees' shadows as raw material. The faces I mimic as much as possible in the firelight for some; for others I leave them blank and faceless. Then when I have a dozen of these shadow soldiers ready to release and expand, I gesture to my friends that it is time to move toward the woods again.

I set the doppelgangers loose. We don't get far before the camp soldiers find their shadowy counterparts and a new cry of alarm goes up. My shadow warriors are fierce and loyal, and they will do what they can to lead the guards on a merry chase and keep them from following us. Then when the morning light comes, they will go back to the trees where they belong.

Chaos descends. Stuck in the middle of the camp, we watch them battle and see how the guards, unable to understand the shadow soldiers, accidentally begin to fight each other in the darkness.

Then a sharp howl splits the night in two, and a new shape appears at the edge of the woods. Dark shadowed eyes flash and a monstrous form throws itself into the fray.

Cold hits me like a bucket of water while Lucas and his family gape.

Dar has found us.

CHAPTER TWENTY-FIVE

I watch in horror as Dar, all snapping teeth and flailing limbs, brushes guards aside with one long, clawed arm.

It's the perfect opportunity to flee. I could not have asked for a better distraction. We could hurry away, leaving nothing but chaos in our wake. But I can't allow her to hurt any more people, not even Lady Aisling's men. Who knows how many she injured when I fled from her the first time. And I certainly can't let her roam free when she's done.

"What is *that*?" whispers Lucas. My gut twists. I am finished with lies and half-truths. Besides, I only said them at Dar's insistence; had I known she was feeding off them, things might have gone very differently.

I swallow hard. "It's Dar, my shadow. Or she was my shadow. I—I thought she was my friend. She convinced me to perform a ritual that made her flesh again."

Lucas's eyes widen. "*You* did that?"

I hang my head. "She was a lost soul. She talked to me and played with me. She was my best friend."

Lucas's mother sighs. "Oh, Emmeline. That's why you hid things from us. You were really hiding her."

Dar morphs into something new, stockier and shorter than her monster form. In minutes she looks like the guards, her face shifting as she dodges and weaves through the shadows and soldiers.

"I must do something about Dar. I can't just let her remain loose, wreaking havoc like this," I say.

She taunts the guards by mirroring their forms, confusing them. But she soon bores of this, and shifts again, this time into something bigger. I shiver.

"I'll help you." Lucas grabs my hand. Heat burns through my fingers.

"But I lied to you. All of you."

Miranda puts a hand on my shoulder. "You came back

for us. You saved our son from Lady Aisling; we will not soon forget that."

"Well, we're not quite safe yet," Alfred says.

"You should go," I say. "I have done enough to your family. I don't want to put any of you in more danger. I'll send some of my shadows with you to keep you hidden."

I glance at my former shadow, and she is monstrous again. Huge horns adorn her head and she uses them to barrel into the guards, sending them scattering into the trees. Behind her, the hint of sunrise stains the sky red. My first thought when I fled her was that I needed help, but now the possibility of my friends getting hurt seems all too real.

"I'm staying," Lucas says. "Maybe my magic can help." He glances at his parents. "But it might be best if you go. Then we won't be distracted trying to save you too."

Alfred shakes his head. "We're not leaving you. But we will stay hidden in Emmeline's shadows between these rocks. We'll be out of the way, I promise."

Lucas gives me an encouraging look. Something warm and light fills my ribs.

"All right. Come on, Lucas," I say. I tie off one end of

the shadows around his parents, then pull the rest tight around me and Lucas. We move quickly from rock to rock trying to get closer without being seen. Some of the soldiers lie on the ground, unmoving, and bile rises in the back of my throat.

We stick to the side of the camp where the soldiers are thinnest. They keep coming back, trying to take Dar down. I wonder if Lady Aisling told them who she really is or if they just know she has shifter magic and would make a valuable prize. They must want to bring her back to Lady Aisling so she can add her to the Garden and devour her talent.

I shudder. I cannot let that happen either.

"We'll have to take care of the soldiers too. We don't want them to come after us until we're safely away," I say.

He nods. "It's almost dawn. I can draw on the light to make bands that will keep them tied up until night falls again, while you go after Dar."

"Will you have enough to work with?"

He squints in the direction of the dawn, and a bright smile blooms on his face. "Definitely. When the sun begins to rise, it takes over the sky quickly. It's already lighter than it was when we left my parents between the boulders."

One look confirms he's right. We both should have enough material to work our craft. Lucas begins to sing, but I keep us concealed behind my shadows for good measure. A few of the guards pause in confusion, unsure where the voice is coming from. Those are the ones Lucas targets first.

The light around us condenses as Lucas crafts it into thin but sturdy bands. A guard's mouth drops open as he watches it form in front of him. He cries out in surprise when the band swoops down to push him back, pinning him against a tree. The guard struggles, but Lucas's work is well-crafted, and he has learned a lot about making his light tangible. The guard will not escape any time soon.

Moments later, two more are pinned against trees by the bright, golden bands. I cast my net of shadows wide and catch several of the guards Dar was toying with at once, then fasten the end to a sturdy tree branch. They hang there, struggling.

That gets Dar's attention.

She turns her huge eyes to me, and her mouth breaks into what I believe is a grin.

"Emmeline," she booms. "I thought I smelled you here."

She stalks toward me, and Lucas tenses at my side. I

weave my shadows in preparation. With every step, Dar's shape changes a little more, a new ear here, a feline twist to her mouth there, spikes jutting out across her spine.

"I told you to run," she says. "Have you come here to help me pick off the guards?" She grins, and it turns my stomach.

"No," I say. "I know you hate the Zinnians and that you have good reason, but I cannot let you hurt them. That is not the answer."

She tilts her head and scowls when she sees Lucas. "What is *he* doing here?"

Behind me, Lucas continues to prepare bands of light, keeping them spinning and waiting in case more guards show up.

"Lucas is my friend."

She looks as though she has been slapped. "No, Emmeline, *I* am your friend."

"Friends do not lie and use each other, Dar. That is not how friendship works."

She snorts. "I beg to differ. Our arrangement worked beautifully for many years. Until he came along." She narrows her eyes at Lucas and stalks toward him. I put myself in the path between them. "What? Are we not friends, Emmeline? We had such plans. You promised me you would never leave me, and I promised the same. I intend to keep my promise."

"I—I do not know what to make of our promises anymore, Dar. You lied so much and so often. I can no longer decide what was true and what was made up. I don't know that you were ever really my friend at all."

"What are you saying?"

"I don't know what was true, but I know I can't let you hurt anyone else. This has to stop."

"Your talent created me. You set me free, Emmeline. Why would I ever want to stop? I have never felt this free before!" Dar spins and takes off at a run.

I pull the big shadows first then the little ones from the saplings and ferns and bushes. Quickly, I weave them together to form a net, putting more of my power into it than ever before. It must hold, I must make them solid enough to stop this madness. The net remains small as I weave it, but it has ample shadow material to expand when I cast it.

Dar whoops and races around the glade, then begins to toy with one of the soldiers pinned to a tree by Lucas's light bands. The man flinches and struggles against his bonds, but they hold fast. With my breath stuttering on my lips, I send the shadow net flying toward Dar. She howls when it hits her, interrupting her fun. When she realizes what I've done, she begins to shout and shake the tightly woven sides.

"Let me out! Let. Me. Out!" she screams, flailing inside the shadow net.

I pull the ends of the net tight, tying it off, then securing my end around a tree. Dar should not be able to wander off easily now.

"Emmeline!" howls Dar. "I thought we were friends." Betrayal glints in her monstrous eyes, and I flinch. Sorrow squeezes my chest, making it hard to breathe.

"I thought we were too. But a friend wouldn't have used me like that."

"Used you? No, I loved you like a sister. I knew you, better than you know yourself." Suddenly Dar ceases her struggles and flashes a grin that makes my stomach hit the ground. Then her hands begin to shift into treacherously sharp claws. I take a step back, and Lucas follows suit. She tears into the material, and though it reforms shortly after every attempt to slice, it isn't fast enough. To my horror, she manages to get a grip on my shadow net and rips it apart. She steps back into the glade, looking for all the world like a cat who just swallowed a bird.

I lean close and whisper to Lucas as we back away from Dar's slowly advancing form. "We have to trap her somehow. I bet a cage of shadows would be stronger if we added bars of your light. We've both done well making our shadows and light tangible, and Dar's new form was born from shadows after all. Maybe that would hold her better than my talent alone. What do you think?"

"The two of our talents combined? Unstoppable." He squeezes my hand, and I almost feel as unstoppable as he believes we might be together.

"Then let's do it." This time, we break into a run, startling Dar and making her pause. Lucas sends a burst of light at her, while my shadows snake toward her. But she evades them both, dodging like she can read our minds.

"We have to get closer," I say. We chase her through the glade as she leaps from rock to rock and climbs from tree to tree.

But then something new sprouts from her shoulders: long, leathery wings. They grow at an alarming rate, then expand. She runs faster, wings ready to take off.

My heart climbs into my throat. If she flies away, I'll never catch her. I may never see her again. I throw the new shadow net I've been pulling together wide and high, imbuing the shadows with as much self-direction and mass as I can muster.

The shadows fold around her, tangling with her wings and bringing her back down to the earth. She hits the ground with a thud and a cry, then transforms yet again. Every second she becomes smaller and shorter, and more human-like. Lucas spins his light, preparing to add it to the shadows holding her in. He gives a quick nod signaling that he is ready.

Finally, Dar stops changing and rises to her feet.

A scream strangles in my throat.

My own dark eyes gaze back at me. She is even wearing the same clothes, the purple dress Miranda bought me.

"You can't hurt me, Emmeline. I am part of you. The voice on your shoulder. The part of you that longs to do naughty things. I *am* you."

I shudder, frozen and completely unable to stop staring at her.

"You are *not* Emmeline!" Lucas cries, sending his light

bands around the shadow net. They draw it up, bolstering and strengthening, like gleaming golden threads intertwining with my dark shadow ropes.

Dar turns a hand into a claw and reaches out to grab one but can't tear through the combined magic. Relief spills over me, but we're not done yet. Together Lucas and I fashion a cage from his bands of light and my ropes of shadow, one that won't let more than a hand through. There is no lock, no door, no exit.

No escape.

Dar screams and rails against our crafted cage. This time, she cannot move it. It does not budge an inch.

She stops and tries a different tack. "Emmeline," she pleads. "Don't do this. Remember how I sang to you whenever you were sad? All the games we would play? All the fun we had, you and me and our shadows? The whole world could belong to us." She lowers her voice to a whisper. "I can set it right. You know I can. That's why you released me. You want to set things right. Everything can go back to how it used to be. Just you and me, Emmeline. Let me out, and everything will be right again."

My mouth is useless as I'm flooded with memories. The two of us and the shadows, that was all I believed I needed.

But when Lucas slips his warm hand in mine and squeezes, I realize she's wrong. She isn't the only one I need, not anymore.

Dar wails in protest and begins to shrink.

Immediately, I close my web of shadows so her small size won't allow her to slip through, and Lucas does the same with his light bands. She is trying to escape this way, but we can't allow it.

She shrinks to the size of a doll, but even then the light and shadow combine to form an unbreakable cage around her. When she tries to grow again, she can't. There is no space, and our shadow and light will not break or bend for her.

She screams in frustration, then sinks to the floor of the cage and begins to cry like a sad, pitiful doll.

"What are you going to do with me?" she whines. "You're such fools. I know your conscience won't let you abandon me here, but if you take me with you, Lady Aisling will never stop hunting you. You will never rest easy again."

I glance at Lucas. I hadn't thought quite that far yet. I only knew I needed to stop her.

"She can come with us," Miranda says, startling us all. They must have come out when they could see the danger had passed. "You both can. We won't let Lady Aisling have either of you."

EPILOGUE

This morning I wake up in a new cottage, one that is white sandstone with gaily painted blue windows and trim, that overlooks the sea. Until we moved here a few days ago, I had never seen the sea before, only read about it in books. It is so vast and endless and beautiful that each morning when the sun rises over it, painting the sky in a rainbow array of colors, it warms me straight to the core.

I pull on my slippers—new ones that Miranda made just for me—and head downstairs for breakfast. I can already smell Lucas toasting croissants.

Lucas's family moved here, the coast of Abbacho, after we finally ended Dar's rampage and routed Lady Aisling's soldiers. I feel more at home here than I ever did on my own parents' estate. Someday I'll have to go back and face them. But for now, I'm welcome to remain here as long as I'd like. Every day, Lucas and I hone our magic together on the beach below our cliffside cottage, weaving shadows and singing light, our magic swirling together and forming something new and special.

I finally know what it's like to really have a friend. It is all I've ever wanted.

Lucas has just finished cooking breakfast when I reach the kitchen and take a seat, snatching a piping hot croissant for myself. Lucas nudges my foot under the table.

"After breakfast we should go to the beach and see if we can catch any fish with a light lure on one of your shadow ropes, and—"

Miranda laughs. "Just don't forget we need to grow a new garden. I'll need your help this afternoon, so don't get too tuckered out before that."

Lucas nods his agreement, but gives me a sly look across the table. I smile back. We intend to use every ounce of energy we have on our talents today. Using them freely now feels like a right, like a bit of rebellion against the Lady who would steal them from us.

"Oh, but first, I must take this upstairs." I finish off my breakfast, grab an extra plate, and march up the stairs. This time, I do not stop on the second floor where our rooms are. I go up another flight of stairs, this one older, but less worn. At the very top is a small door. I take a key from a chain around my neck and unlock the door, the gears grinding in protest. When I open it, I breathe out in relief.

The shadow-and-light cage is still there, taking up most of the floor, and so is its occupant. The rest of the room is sparse, a few extra pieces of furniture shoved into one corner, covered by a sheet. A table in front of a window that looks out on the ocean, just waiting for someone to set a vase of flowers upon it.

Dar's form is an unnerving one she has taken often lately: she looks just like me—same height, hair, face, and even clothes—but with a strange, unhinged glint in her eyes. Her fingers clench and unclench around an unseen object as she prowls, but when she sees me in the doorway, she launches herself at the alternating shadow and light bars forming her cage. The shadows alone, she could cut or squeeze through, but Lucas and I crafted one that filled up the spaces so she can't squeeze through the bands. It has held for weeks, and while we're prepared to reinforce it if necessary, I believe it will remain intact for quite some time. I test the strength of the bars every morning, and each time, they are as strong as the day we made them.

Dar watches me as I cross the room, mirroring every motion and expression I make as though she is still my shadow. It is more than unnerving. When I stop at her cage, she stops too, and stares at me unblinking. It is disconcerting to have to face myself every morning like this, but she is my responsibility.

"My pretty little friend," she coos at me. "Let me out, please, I will be good, I promise."

I shake my head. "I'm sorry, but I just don't trust you." I slide the plate through the bars, then reseal the bonds.

Her face twists. "Cruel mistress. I thought you said you would not hurt anyone else in my name. What do you call this?" She spits at me as she talks. Her words pinch my chest, but I swallow it down.

"Enjoy your breakfast, Dar," I say, then turn my back to her. She bangs her fists against the bars, but they do not move.

"She is coming for us, you know. And she'll take Lucas too. If you set me free, I can protect you from her."

I glance over my shoulder at her. "It will be a long time before Lady Aisling finds us here. Zinnia does not have a treaty with Abbacho. We are safe for now."

A sly grin breaks over Dar's—my—face. "Do you really believe that will stop her?"

I walk away, doing my best to stop myself from shuddering. The truth is, no, I do not believe it will stop her. But at least it buys us some time.

"Let me out! Don't you walk away! LET. ME. OUT!" she screams after me, but I duck out of the attic room and lock the door behind me.

We can't set her loose. She is too dangerous. Perhaps once she was a kind person who happened to have a talent. Then Lady Aisling's siphon magic broke her into pieces. It made her vicious and unstable. But I cared for Dar once, and I'll continue to protect her as long as I can, even from herself.

For now, we are safe, but Lady Aisling is out there, and she knows who we are. She'll be looking for us. When she finds us again, this time, we will be ready.

ACKNOWLEDGMENTS

———◦———

I'm so grateful for the opportunity to launch my second series with *Shadow Weaver* and for all the people who've encouraged and supported this project from the very beginning. And of course, you, my readers—you're the reason I write!

Behind every good book is an excellent team and support system, and this one is no exception. I would especially like to thank those noted below:

My editor, Annie Berger, and the entire team at Sourcebooks, for making me feel so welcome. Your enthusiasm is infectious! I'm so thrilled that I get to work with you all and that this series found such a wonderful home.

My agent, Suzie Townsend, for being my biggest cheer-leader through book proposal after book proposal until I finally happened upon just the right idea. And for providing the perfect spark of inspiration about the true nature of Lady Aisling! Thank you so much for all that you do.

Mindy McGinnis, Riley Redgate, Amy Trueblood, and Rachel Simon for reading early drafts of this book and challenging me to make my shadow girl shine.

The lovely folks who regularly attend the Boston Writer meet-ups—I've said it before and I'll say it again, but the crepes and commiseration are truly invaluable. Thanks for listening during that long year of trying to sell another book.

And finally, Jason and our fur babies Tootsie, Milo, and Teddy—because I always save the best for last.

ABOUT THE AUTHOR

MarcyKate Connolly is a *New York Times* bestselling children's book author and nonprofit administrator living in New England with her husband and pugs. She's also a caffeine addict and a voracious reader. You can visit her online at marcykate.com.